The
Sewing Shop

De-ann Black

Other books in the Sewing, Crafts & Quilting series are:

Book 1 - The Sewing Bee
Book 2 - The Sewing Shop

Paperback edition published 2021

The Sewing Shop

ISBN: 9798512072868

Also by De-ann Black (Romance, Action/Thrillers & Children's books). See her Amazon Author page or website for further details about her books, screenplays, illustrations, art and fabric designs.
www.De-annBlack.com

Romance:

The Dressmaker's Cottage
The Sewing Shop
Heather Park
The Tea Shop by the Sea
The Bookshop by the Seaside
The Sewing Bee
The Quilting Bee
Snow Bells Wedding
Snow Bells Christmas
Summer Sewing Bee
The Chocolatier's Cottage
Christmas Cake Chateau
The Beemaster's Cottage
The Sewing Bee By The Sea
The Flower Hunter's Cottage

The Christmas Knitting Bee
The Sewing Bee & Afternoon Tea
The Vintage Sewing & Knitting Bee
Shed In The City
The Bakery By The Seaside
Champagne Chic Lemonade Money
The Christmas Chocolatier
The Christmas Tea Shop & Bakery
The Vintage Tea Dress Shop In Summer
Oops! I'm The Paparazzi
The Bitch-Proof Suit

Action/Thrillers:

Love Him Forever.
Someone Worse.
Electric Shadows.

The Strife Of Riley.
Shadows Of Murder.

Children's books:

Faeriefied.
Secondhand Spooks.
Poison-Wynd.

Wormhole Wynd.
Science Fashion.
School For Aliens.

Colouring books:

Summer Garden. Spring Garden. Autumn Garden. Sea Dream.
Festive Christmas. Christmas Garden. Flower Bee. Wild Garden.
Faerie Garden Spring. Flower Hunter. Stargazer Space. Bee Garden.

Embroidery books:

Floral Nature Embroidery Designs
Scottish Garden Embroidery Designs

Contents

CHAPTER ONE

Iona looked out the window of the quilt shop as she arranged the new fabric display. There was no sign of the mystery man she'd been watching the past few days.

Early morning sunlight shone on the windows of the shops opposite — the bakers, grocers, and the shop that had been closed and shuttered since she'd arrived last week. The shop that belonged to the elusive man. Every day since she'd started her new job at the quilt shop, there was talk about the man who'd taken over the empty shop beside the bakers. No one knew what type of shop he was intending to open as he kept his plans, and himself, a secret. Usually, in a friendly little community like this one, where everyone knew everyone else's business, his shop plans would be gossiped about. Instead, the gossip circulated about the mystery man.

Few people had even glimpsed him, but she'd seen him every morning when he appeared to measure the outside of his shop — for a sign above the front window presumably, and contemplate the overall look of it.

Originally a sweet shop, it was painted pastel pink and had a pretty pink and white striped canopy, but the shop had been long closed.

No one knew anything about him. But he was handsome. She knew that for sure. Her heart beat faster every time she glimpsed his tall, fit figure in the mornings. Once, he'd glanced across at the quilt shop, as if sensing he was being watched. She'd hid behind one of the quilts on display and peered out surreptitiously. He'd stared over at the quilt shop's front window with eyes that seemed to know she was watching him. His handsome face looked tense, then he'd hurried into his shop and locked the door. Maybe he was letting her know he knew she was watching him. The only person in the village to see the mystery man.

He dressed very well, stylish. There was nothing casual about this man. He wore dark trousers and classic shirts, usually with a waistcoat. She estimated that he was in his mid thirties. He had light brown hair and a seriously handsome face, and it was difficult to fathom what type of business he was in. With his shirt sleeves rolled up when he was standing on a ladder measuring the fascia for a sign, he could've passed for a well–dressed handyman, especially as he had a white van that was parked nearby. And yet, he didn't quite fit that category. No, he was skilled at something else, but what? She'd dated a chef in her patchwork of disastrous relationships, and she wondered if this was his plan — to open a tea shop, or classy cafe or some sort of patisserie establishment. Or maybe he was an artist and planned to open a gallery.

But there was no sign of him this morning. No hint of movement in his shop at all.

Iona piled the fat quarter quilting fabric bundles in the display, added thread to match the colour themes of the floral prints, and concentrated on making the display look enticing. Then she unlocked the front door and opened the shop for business. For a moment, she stepped outside and breathed in the fresh air. The sunny morning brightened everything.

Pink spring blossom lingered on the trees that were dotted along the village's main street even though it was the beginning of summer. But high up in the Scottish Highlands the seasons had a mind of their own.

The quilt shop job was temporary, for a few weeks during the summer to help with the quilt orders and embroidery kits. Iona, single and in her early thirties, was a quilter from one of the large towns on the East Coast of Scotland, and when she heard of the vacancy in the little quilt shop that was situated in a quaint village in the Highlands, she'd applied for the position and been successful.

Iona was a temporary replacement for Eevie while she was away on business in London with her new boyfriend, one of the local men. The quilt shop was part of the village community of cottages and small shops, and was a former cottage converted into a shop selling quilts, fabric and yarn. They also sold floral theme embroidery kits. The kits were a fairly recent addition to the shop, and their popularity, especially for their online orders, was one of the reasons why Jinette, the shop's owner, needed an assistant.

Iona left little behind her when she moved to the village — mainly a scattering of broken dreams, broken promises and broken relationships. She was looking on the summer job as a working holiday, somewhere she could enjoy quilting while earning a living and planning what she wanted to do instead of being stuck in a rut.

2

She loved living in the accommodation at the back of the shop. There was a bedroom, a tiny kitchen and bathroom, and a cosy living room with a real log fire. A warm summer was promised, but the weather could be unpredictable up north, so if it rained or felt cold one night, she planned to light the logs and enjoy the cosiness of an evening drinking hot chocolate and sewing quilts by the fireside.

The cottage had a back garden and she liked sitting outside in the early evenings breathing in the scent of the flowers. It was a pretty garden, slightly untamed, which somehow matched her personality. She wasn't wild by any means, but moving to the village, stepping out of the safe rut she'd been in for so long, felt a bit adventurous.

She'd lived in a tiny rented flat, and appreciated being able to step out into a garden. The cottage accommodation was everything she could've hoped for. The vintage styling was mixed with floral prints on the curtains and home decor items. She slept under a beautiful pink patchwork quilt and loved how the sun shone in the shop window every day, making her world feel like it was less in shadow and filled with a sunny fresh start.

She realised that living in the converted cottage meant she was never away from her work, but for a quilt lover like her, being surrounded by shelves piled with wonderful fabric, a haberdashery brimming with gorgeous thread, sewing quilts and making new friends, it was perfect. The only downside was the thought that she'd have to leave when the summer was over, but as this was the start of the summertime, she pushed the thought of leaving to the back of her mind and enjoyed working in the quilt shop.

The local sewing bee was held twice a week in the shop or at the local laird's mansion hotel. For the summer, with the mansion being busy with holiday guests, the sewing bee nights were being held in the shop. She planned to start sewing a patchwork quilt at the bee that evening. She was still getting to know everyone and the sewing bee nights were ideal for quilting and chatting.

As Iona went back into the shop she saw Jinette walking towards her. Jinette lived in a cottage further along the main street. She'd owned the quilt shop for years. She was in her fifties, an adept quilter, experienced in all types of sewing, including embroidery and dressmaking, and a fine knitter.

'Morning, Iona,' Jinette said, bustling into the shop, smiling, armed with a bag of fruit scones from the bakers for their morning

3

tea break. Jinette usually wore skirts and blouses she'd made herself, and being in her company had given Iona the impetus to wear something other than jeans and a top. Iona's slim build suited the ditsy print dress she was wearing, one of the few dresses she'd sewn herself.

'Morning. I've put the new fabric bundles in the window display,' Iona told her.

'Great idea. That was fast work. You must've been working late or up with the dawn to get all those bundles cut.'

'A bit of both. I'm enjoying living in the cottage. It's such a change from the flat I was sharing. And I think it's all the fresh air and being happy surrounded by fabric and quilts that makes getting up early a pleasure.'

'There's nothing better than loving what you do for a living. Speaking of which, the packaging for the new embroidery kits should arrive later this morning, so look out for a delivery.'

Iona wasn't an expert embroiderer, but she was keen to advance her skills, and being in the company of Jinette and other local ladies who were brilliant at embroidery was sure to help her learn more stitches and improve her techniques.

'Remember, the sewing bee is on tonight,' Jinette reminded her. 'So pace yourself during the day.'

Iona laughed. 'You make it sound as if I'll need a burst of energy to deal with the sewing bee.'

Jinette smiled and nodded. 'You'll see what I mean. You were still getting settled in last week, so we kept things calm. But tonight you'll find out what a lively evening we have. So be prepared to stitch until you drop.'

'I think I can handle that.' Iona ran her hand along one of the new fabric bundles. 'My name is on this one. I'm planning to make a new patchwork quilt. The blues and fresh floral prints are gorgeous. I love forget–me–nots and love–in–a–mist.'

Jinette eyed the fabric bundle. 'Those new prints are lovely. Once the women see them, they'll buy them up instantly, so you'll need to get up early again to cut a load more.'

'It's such a busy little shop. I knew it would be fairly busy with it being the only quilt shop in the area, but the online sales are crazy. I didn't expect to have to pack up so many orders every day. We must be responsible for keeping the post office going.'

'There's a courier service that picks up our customer orders two or three times a week, depending on their schedule. Having a website has made such a difference to things. Before, we relied almost exclusively on local sales and tourist purchases. Now, we're supplying orders to all sorts of far flung places. It's been a great thing. Which reminds me, I'll have to update the website with the new fabric bundles.'

Jinette flicked on the shop's computer, then went through to the kitchen to make their morning tea.

Iona gazed thoughtfully out the shop's front window. 'Have you heard any more gossip about our mystery man?'

'Apparently he's opening his shop soon, but we don't know when. You're the only one to have had a proper look at him. I hope he's as handsome as you've described,' Jinette called through to her.

'It's not that I'm attracted to him or anything like that,' Iona said in her defence.

Jinette popped her head round the door and gave Iona a disbelieving look.

'Okay,' Iona relented. 'He's easy on the eye.'

'According to you he's gorgeous. The best looking man you've ever seen. Including Hollywood heartthrobs.'

'Did I say that?'

'You did. I have witnesses. Customers heard you while you were wrapping their fabric orders. Now it's local gossip. We're all waiting to see if he's even half as handsome as you've described.'

'He's bound to be a let down. Someone always is when they're lauded to be outstanding.'

Jinette sighed as she continued to make the tea. 'Maybe it'll be nice to have a handsome man working in his shop opposite us. A pleasant view.'

Iona thought the view was pleasant enough. A traditional, quaint niche in the Highlands with trees lining the street, rolling hills and a nearby loch that she'd yet to visit. Picturesque perfection.

'He may not be single,' Iona reminded Jinette.

Jinette brought their buttered fruit scones through and put them on the counter. 'It doesn't stop us from dreaming though, does it?'

Iona set their chairs up, ready for tea, scones and a chat before work. 'I suppose not, but what if he finds out that we're secretly swooning over him?'

Jinette laughed. 'Swooning? I haven't swooned since...I can't remember when—'

'Since you met me,' Lochty announced, overhearing their conversation as he hurried in carrying a bunch of fresh flowers for Jinette. Lochty was a well–built, mature man with a bushy beard and was a stalwart of the local community.

Jinette had recently started dating Lochty, though she denied they were an item yet. Just friends with the promise of benefits. He'd loved her for as long as he could remember, missed his chance when she married someone else, then waited a reasonable amount of time after she was widowed to make his intentions known. Though his intentions were always obvious. Subtlety wasn't in Lochty's nature.

Jinette smiled when he gave her the flowers.

'I got them from Kier. He's out doing his rounds delivering fresh flowers to customers,' Lochty explained. 'I know you like roses.'

Jinette breathed in the scent of the flowers. 'I'll put them in a vase. They'll look nice in the window display.'

While Jinette and Lochty disappeared into the kitchen, Iona noticed the mystery man leave his shop and stride up the street.

'Jinette! Quick. Mystery man's on the move. Come and have a look at him,' Iona called to her.

Jinette and Lochty came running through and peered out the window beside Iona.

'Where is he?' Jinette asked her.

Iona pointed further along the street. 'He's hurrying away there, near where you live.'

Neither of them saw him.

'I'll track him down,' said Lochty, and hurried out of the quilt shop.

They watched Lochty speed walking after him.

Jinette bit her lip and then looked straight at Iona. 'This is your chance.'

'For what?'

'To nosey in his window while he's out.'

Iona's stomach knotted nervously. 'I'm not sure. Besides, his windows are shuttered. I won't be able to see inside.'

Jinette grabbed a leaflet from the embroidery kits display and thrust it into Iona's reluctant hands. 'Stick this through his letterbox. Take your time and have a wee ogle through at his shop.'

Realising this was a prime opportunity to find out what was inside his shop, Iona swallowed her reluctance and began to see things from Jinette's perspective.

'We'll never get a better chance to nosey,' Jinette said encouragingly. 'And you're a faster runner than me.'

Iona eye–balled her. 'You left Lochty eating your dust when he was chasing you to your cottage the other night.'

Jinette fluffed her cardigan and brushed a few strands of hair that had broken free from her chignon. 'That was just a bit of fun.'

'But you were fast, Jinette.'

'I was fast on my feet when I was a girl,' Jinette admitted. 'Maybe I've still got some racing days in me, but this morning, on your marks, Iona. Run.'

Nodding firmly, Iona took a deep breath and hurried over to the shuttered shop, armed with the leaflet. The premises was another cottage converted years ago into a small sweet shop at the front and accommodation at the back.

Her heart thundered with nervous excitement as she viewed his front window up close. He'd shuttered every gap. No peep holes at all. So she bent down, lifted the letterbox and peered in.

At that moment, a man's voice spoke behind her and startled her.

'You're about to get caught.'

Iona jumped, almost trapped her fingers in the letterbox as she stuffed the leaflet through and pulled her hands away as if she'd been burned. She glanced round and saw the tall figure of a man staring down at her with beautiful grey eyes filled with accusation. She barely came up to his shoulders.

'I was just delivering a promotional leaflet advertising our new embroidery kits.' She tried to sound confident even though her first instinct was to make a run for it back to the quilt shop.

'Don't tell lies, Iona.'

He knew her name! This startled her even more.

He wasn't the mystery man. Oh no, this man had a shock of blond hair and could rival the mystery man in the handsomeness stakes. His face was gorgeous, and those grey eyes were filled with assurance that he knew she was up to no good.

She felt the colour rush to her cheeks. He wasn't much older than her, but his manly confidence was evident. And he had such a sexy appearance. He wore rich, dark blue cords that clung to every muscle

7

of his long legs. His sky blue shirt emphasised his broad shoulders and lean waist. Open at the neck, it exposed a hint of pale golden skin that looked like he'd been out in the sunshine shirtless. Her heart fluttered excitedly. This man was model material. His closeness disconcerted her.

'Smile,' he whispered. 'My name is Kier.'

'*Kier*?' Jinette and a few other women had warned her about him. A sweet talking heartbreaker. Joy of joys, she had to have been caught by him.

He saw her reaction to his name, and smirked with lips that tempted her to kiss him and run her hands over his clean shaven jaw. He smelled delicious, as if freshly showered, and had a hint of masculine bergamot scent.

'You're the...*flower grower*,' Iona said hesitantly.

'You were going to say something else, weren't you? But if it's my reputation you're worried about, I'd put that aside because right now your mystery man is heading this way. Judging by the unamused look on his face, he saw you spying through his letterbox.'

Everything seemed to happen so fast, and the fluttering of her heart confused her. Kier had a reputation for being extremely handsome, a walking temptation, and although she was worried about her current predicament, she couldn't deny the effect he had on her. Standing so close to her, he seemingly wanted to rescue her — and was prepared to accept that she'd been lying to him.

She felt the need to sweep her shoulder–length, light auburn hair back from her face, and wished she'd bothered with her makeup rather than given her green eyes just a flick of mascara and her pretty face a hint of blusher.

Kier focussed all his attention on her. He'd seen her a few times since she'd arrived, but they'd yet to be introduced. He thought she was very attractive and had asked acquaintances if she was single. But at the moment, there was something else to deal with. The new shop owner was getting closer by the second. While out delivering his flowers, he'd seen the man leaving the shop and then quickly coming back. Iona was about to be confronted by him.

Kier raised his voice and smiled at Iona. 'I thought we could have a picnic lunch up at the loch. Make an afternoon of it. What do you say? Will I buy your favourite from the bakers — a bridie or are you up for a cheese and onion puff?'

'A bridie,' she heard herself reply, sounding shrill.

'I think I'll join you.' He smiled and whispered. 'Say thank you, Kier.'

Iona smiled tightly, especially as she saw the mystery man looming near, heading straight for them. 'Thank you, Kier.'

'Have you finished delivering all your leaflets?' Kier asked loud enough for the man to overhear.

'I have. Jinette has the kettle on for our morning tea. So I'd better go back there now.' She went to scurry away, but Kier put his arm around her shoulders, anchoring her to him, and gave her a squeeze as if they were a couple.

'I think I'll join you for a cuppa.' Kier accompanied her across to the quilt shop seconds before the man arrived outside his shop.

'That was close,' Jinette said, looking like she'd been urging them not to get caught.

Kier stepped inside the quilt shop and shook his head at Iona. 'That was your plan? To peek through his letterbox when he was only up the road?'

'It was my idea,' Jinette confessed.

Kier continued to shake his head at Iona. 'But you went along with the crazy plan. Because it was crazy. That was silly of you.'

Jinette wasn't fussed about any scolding Kier felt he was due to give out. She wanted to know only one thing. 'Did you see inside his shop?'

Iona's breathing was still ragged from nervous excitement, partly due to being within close range of Kier. 'I did.'

The colour drained from Jinette's flushed cheeks. She knew from the tone of Iona's voice that whatever she saw wasn't something great. 'What type of shop is he opening?'

'A sewing shop. I saw roles of fabric, piles of quilting fabric bundles, dress fabric, thread, everything that would make him our rival.' Iona took a deep breath. 'I think that's the reason why he's been sneaky. He must've known we wouldn't be happy having another sewing and fabric shop right across from us.'

CHAPTER TWO

Over tea, Iona and Jinette discussed what to do about their rival.

Kier left to continue his flower deliveries, but had promised to help in any way he could.

Iona cupped her tea and gazed out the window as she watched Kier walk back to where he'd parked his classy SUV. Such a tall, handsome man, she thought, wishing that she really was going to have lunch with him up at the loch.

'Kier's a handsome one, isn't he?' Jinette said, noticing Iona's interest in him.

There was no point in denying it. 'He is. He's the walking temptation you and the other ladies warned me about. But I was glad he stepped in to help me avoid being caught peering through our rival's letterbox.'

'Kier has a good heart. It's just that...well, he's got a reputation for being a heartbreaker. I wouldn't want to see you hurt because of him. Of course, maybe a wee summer fling would be a nice distraction from work.'

'I'm not really the summer fling, or any fling, type.'

'If Kier invites you up to see his flowers, you should go. He lives in the farmhouse that's part of his estate. He's wealthy in his own right, and grows lovely flowers in his fields. It's a beautiful estate.'

'He pretended for Aran's benefit that we were going to have a picnic lunch at the loch. Does he own the land near there?'

'No, that's owned by the local laird. He's the owner of the mansion hotel, and he's away on business.' Jinette paused and looked thoughtful. 'But maybe Kier will ask you to have lunch with him for real. I saw him gazing at you.'

Iona tried not to blush. 'I'm sure with Kier being rich and handsome he has plenty of women eager for his attention.'

'I dare say he has, but I haven't heard of him dating anyone recently. In fact, when I think about it, his reputation for being a bit of a womaniser could be on the wane.' Jinette smiled. 'I like Kier, even though sometimes he's a rascal.'

'In what way?'

Jinette shrugged. 'He knows he's a looker, and when he wants to smooth things over, I've seen him flirt his way into the good books of various women. But I suppose no one ever really gets hurt. He's never seriously dated any of the local women. All we've heard is that when he went away to the cities on business, he became involved with women there.'

'Did Kier admit to this?'

'Not in so many words, no, but...well, you know, a fine young man in the city. He's bound to have had a few flings.'

Iona nodded, and then thought about Kier warning her about Aran. 'He didn't need to help me today. He could've let me get caught noseying in Aran's shop.'

'He could have, yes, but I think he likes you.'

Iona felt the blush rise in her cheeks. 'It's been so long since I've dated anyone, and certainly never any man as attractive as Kier,' she admitted.

'Romance is wonderful when you find the right man, but tricky when you date the wrong types. Unfortunately, quite a few of us pick the wrong ones.'

'I've certainly made a few mistakes.' Iona reeled them off. 'The cheating chef, the lying accountant, the two–timing business manager...' Iona sighed. 'It's not a long list, and I'm not into flings, but I've definitely not been lucky in love.'

'Luck can change in a heartbeat. As long as you're open to romance. Don't let the past sour the present.'

Iona nodded. It was good advice.

Movement from across the road interrupted their conversation. Jinette had phoned Lochty to tell him what had happened, and he'd gone off to get on with his own work for the day. But now the new shop's owner was striding towards the quilt shop, armed with the embroidery promotion leaflet.

Iona gasped when she saw their rival approach. 'Oh no, here he comes. And he's not smiling.'

Jinette clutched at the top button of her cardigan. 'We've got three choices. Run and hide, confront him outside, or invite him in for tea.'

Iona wasn't in the mood to hide or try to tame him with tea and smiles. 'Option two gets my vote.'

Jinette nodded firmly in agreement. 'Shall we?'

11

Iona met Jinette's determined gaze and together they stepped outside the shop to confront him.

He stopped a short distance from them, seemingly surprised by their challenging attitude.

He hadn't expected them to do this. He hadn't even intended coming over. But after picking up the leaflet that Iona had dropped through, reading it, wondering if his suspicions were unfounded, he'd checked out their website — again. Several times he'd read through Jinette's introduction to the shop's website, and the recent welcoming post she'd written about Iona being a temporary assistant. Yes, he'd trawled their website. Every item they stocked, he'd studied and compared to his own, not through menace, through trying to find a way to prevent them from being rivals. But Iona's barefaced cheek, peering through his letterbox, unsettled him, so he'd decided that with his opening due the following day, he'd have to talk to them. Then again, Kier made him doubt his suspicions. Perhaps Iona was only posting a leaflet? Either way, he needed to talk to the quilt shop women.

'If you're coming over to cause trouble,' Jinette announced, 'you can turn around and head back to your shop right now.'

He held up the leaflet. 'I saw Iona drop this through my letterbox.'

Iona was taken aback. Did everyone know her name?

'And I saw her peering in, having a look inside my shop.' He glared accusingly at her.

'I did not,' Iona lied. 'Your letterbox was stiff. I was just trying to stuff the leaflet through.'

Her strong denial make him pause and take a deep breath. 'Before we go any further, perhaps I should introduce myself. I'm Aran, and I recently inherited the shop. It belonged to my great aunt, but I didn't know she remembered me. I haven't seen her since I was a boy, and barely only a few times even then. Apparently, I'm her only remaining relative. I'm living in the cottage until I buy a house in the village.'

'I'm Jinette, and this is Iona.' Jinette introduced them sounding blunt.

'You should also know that I've seen your website and I'm aware of the type of quilt shop you have and what you sell,' he stated clearly.

'If you weren't hiding behind your shuttered shop front, maybe we could say the same thing about you,' Iona chided him.

Aran swallowed a sharp retort. He conceded that she was right.

'You have an advantage over us,' Jinette told him. 'So I'll ask you outright — are you opening up a sewing shop?'

'I am.' The muscles in his handsome face tightened as he said this.

'Why would you do that?' Iona couldn't help sounding shrill. 'Surely you knew this could be detrimental to our business.'

He sighed heavily. 'I can explain.' His hazel eyes viewed them, ready to defend his actions.

Jinette and Iona's expression showed they were less than interested in hearing his excuses.

He continued anyway. 'I ran a sewing shop in Edinburgh from my house. I was planning to secure premises because of the success of my sales. I sell fabric for dressmaking and quilting. I also sell quilts I've made, some items of clothing, including dresses and skirts, waistcoats and shirts, but mainly quilts. And fabric, including quilt fabric bundles.' He glanced at the bundles on display in their window.

'That sounds like we're firm rivals,' said Jinette, trying to hide how upset she was. Confronting this man wasn't something she'd planned to do.

'In the past, I'd have said yes,' he replied. 'But given the fact that both of us sell more from our online stores than our brick and mortar shops, I don't think we are.'

Iona and Jinette exchanged a glance, considering if they agreed.

'I agree up to a point,' Jinette conceded. 'But we still rely on local sales, including visitors and tourist trade. That's something we will clash over.'

'Perhaps we can come to some sort of...agreement,' he ventured.

Iona's green eyes narrowed suspiciously. She'd heard comments like this from previous employers, ex–boyfriends and others with their own interests as a priority. 'What type of agreement?' She sounded as if he'd have to come up with something pretty convincing.

'I...I'm not sure,' he said hesitantly. 'Maybe we can sit down and discuss it, rather than shout at each other in public.'

Jinette folded her arms across her chest and stood firm. 'I'm fine with public. This is a small, friendly community. We don't have many secrets around here. We've always aimed to help each other, and that comes from being open with each other, rather than sneaking about in the shadows like you've done.'

He took the verbal swipe firmly on the chin. And what a handsome chin it was. Iona loathed thinking he was as good looking up close as she'd assumed he'd be. But her heart didn't flutter, at least not in attraction, only in pent up resentment. She liked Jinette. She liked the quilt shop and everyone she'd met in the village. Now this arrogant man was about to ruin her summer there. The taste of her resentment was indeed bitter.

Aran gazed at Iona, trying not to admire her. She was even prettier than the photo on the website had presented. No wonder she had a handsome boyfriend. Kier was a lucky man...

'Well?' Jinette said, jarring him from his wayward thoughts. 'What type of agreement had you in mind?'

He didn't have an answer. In his mind, he'd thought things would have worked out differently. He'd have opened the shop and then tried to convince them that he'd no intention of trampling over their business.

Jinette shook her head at him. 'No, I didn't think you'd have anything planned.'

'Why don't you just go back to your shop and hide behind your shutters,' Iona challenged him.

'What was I supposed to do?' he said, sounding exasperated. 'I inherited exactly what I needed — a small shop that I could set up as the sewing shop. And it's in this lovely village, with accommodation. Not many people would forgo that opportunity, would they?'

'No, I suppose they wouldn't,' Iona stated. 'But you could've handled things differently. Jinette and the ladies of the sewing bee, and myself, would've probably helped you. Maybe we'd have thought up how we could help each other without clashing in business.'

'I didn't think we'd clash too badly,' he told Iona. 'After all, my sales are mainly from online orders. It doesn't matter if my shop is situated in Edinburgh or here. The customers buy my quilts and fabric from far and wide. If this shop was in the heart of Edinburgh, it wouldn't even affect your business.'

'That's true,' Jinette admitted. 'But you're right across from us. You hadn't even the decency to come over and admit what was going on. We'd no idea what type of shop you were opening.'

'You can imagine the shock Jinette got when I told her it was a sewing shop. I couldn't help noticing all the fabric on the shelves and bundles for quilting,' Iona explained.

'I'm sorry this has come to such an acrimonious discussion,' Aran said, sounding disheartened. 'I'll leave you now, no doubt so you can tear my character to shreds.'

He went to walk away, but Iona shouted after him. 'We're better people than that. So whatever twisted ideas are swirling around in that arrogant mind of yours, you should rethink your attitude. We've been straightforward with you. No business I've ever worked for, especially small shops that deal in fabric and haberdashery, would be so amenable to you.'

He paused and reconsidered. 'Maybe we all need to calm down and rethink our business strategies.'

'My business strategy is quite fine,' Jinette said confidently. 'We're continuing business as usual. If you can think of something helpful to say, you're welcome to come back over anytime, as long as you don't wrap your suggestions in lies.'

Aran nodded firmly. 'I will, as long as Iona doesn't tell lies either.'

And then he walked away.

Iona huffed and stared after him. He'd obviously heard Kier telling her not to tell lies.

'The cheek of him,' Jinette said, loud enough for her voice to carry in the warm air.

His broad shoulders juddered hearing her comment, but he continued on towards his shop, went inside and locked the door.

His laptop was still on the counter, open at the quilt shop's website showing Iona's lovely face smiling out at him. His heart twisted. He hated being the scoundrel in this scenario. He needed a plan. Something to smooth things over. But what...? He had no idea.

He clicked the buttons on his own website, making his new online shop live. Now they could view his shop, the fabric, quilts, all the items he had for sale, and read his bio. Not that this would make them like him. Clearly, he'd caused such a feeling of resentment. The rift would surely never heal.

'Aran's made his shop's website live,' Iona called through to Jinette.

Jinette was in the kitchen making them another pot of tea. They hadn't even touched their scones due to all the upset.

While the kettle boiled, Jinette hurried through and looked over Iona's shoulder as she scrolled through the items listed on his website.

Jinette noticed the name of his shop on the banner headline of his site. 'The Sewing Shop?' She sighed wearily. 'He had all this meticulously planned.'

Iona nodded. 'He's a weasel.'

'He's not as handsome as Kier,' Jinette said snippily.

'No, he's not. He's better looking from a distance. I don't know what I was thinking when I said he was utterly handsome.'

'A sleekit attitude isn't a good look even on the most handsome of faces.'

'No, Jinette, it's not. And I don't trust him at all.'

The kettle clicked off the boil. 'I'll make our tea and we'll discuss our plan of action.'

Iona studied Aran's face. The picture he'd put on his bio showed him looking confident, unsmiling and the type of man you'd rely on if you were ordering things like fabric and quilts. He didn't look dubious. He appeared competent, and from the stylish quilts he was selling, this man could obvious quilt and sewing very well. But she still preferred the quilts that Jinette sold. They were made by Jinette and members of the Sewing Bee. The ladies quilts were beautiful and their fabric choices were lovely.

'I prefer our quilts,' Iona said as Jinette brought their tea through.

They both sat down at the counter and decided to eat their buttered scones while discussing their strategy.

Iona looked thoughtfully at Aran's website. 'We have gorgeous embroidery kits and yarn. He doesn't sell those, so we're already ahead of the game when it comes to knitting and embroidery.'

'I'll embroider some of our new quilts.' Jinette sounded confident.

'Quilt embroidery?' Iona wasn't familiar with this.

16

'Yes, I used to hand stitch my quilts using embroidery techniques. I haven't done that for a while, but I think I'll include that element in some of our quilts.'

'I'd love to learn quilt embroidery.'

'I'll show you. It's easy–peasy. It'll help you learn more embroidery stitches as well. I'll teach you how to satin stitch tiny leaves on your quilts. I used to love that effect.'

Smiling at each other, they ate their scones and drank their tea, feeling that they had a plan of action.

While customers came and went throughout the morning, Jinette showed Iona how to embroider satin stitch leaves on to a quilt.

'I love this effect,' Iona said enthusiastically.

Customers were interested to see these techniques, while buying fabric, thread and yarn from the shop.

'I also like to embroider floral designs on the quilts.' Jinette showed Iona how to create a pretty flower effect.

They were so busy with their quilt embroidery that the morning flew by and by lunchtime Iona had mastered the technique.

'There's always something new to learn when quilting,' said Iona, delighted with her work.

'Let's get some photos of the quilt embroidery to put it on the website,' Jinette suggested.

They were taking the photos when Airlie, one of the sewing bee members, came scurrying in. Airlie was in her forties, a seasoned quilter, and enjoyed wearing bright colours like the turquoise and pink top she was wearing.

Airlie sounded anxious. 'I heard about the argy–bargy you had this morning with Aran. But I wondered if you'd noticed that he's taken down the shutters from his front window.'

Iona and Jinette had been so busy they hadn't noticed and hurried to take a look across at his shop.

'He's only just revealed his window display,' said Airlie. 'I came out of the bakers and there it was. It looks like some sort of sewing shop.'

'It is,' Jinette told her, explaining the events of the morning.

'I'm sorry, Jinette. I didn't want to upset you,' Airlie apologised.

'No, you were right to come over,' Jinette assured her. 'We were engrossed in our quilting'.

'Is the sewing bee still on tonight?' Airlie asked.

'Yes, we're not shelving our bee nights because of the current fiasco with that man,' Jinette said firmly.

'Great, because a few of the ladies have ideas of how to thwart him.'

Jinette and Iona stared at Airlie.

'The gossip is circulating around the village about what he's done, what he's planning, and what we can do to help.'

At that moment, they saw a man heading towards the quilt shop.

'Here's Gairn, the baker's son,' said Airlie. 'Folk were talking about the whole dilemma in the bakers.'

'I haven't seen Gairn in ages. I thought he was studying as a master baker or something like that in Edinburgh,' Jinette remarked.

'He is,' Airlie confirmed. 'He's only here for a wee while during the summer, working with his dad in the baker's shop. He's grown into a fine young man.'

Gairn was around the same age as Kier, but had a tall, lean, rangy build. His dark hair was swept back from a classically good looking face, and his eyes matched the clear blue of the midday sky. He wore baker's whites, and smiled when he noticed them looking out at him. If he hadn't been carrying two large cake boxes he'd have waved in at them.

Jinette opened the shop door. 'Come away in, Gairn. I was just saying that I haven't seen you in ages.'

'You'll be seeing more of me in the autumn. I've nearly finished my baking and confectionery course, then I'm planning on joining my dad in the business.' He put the cake boxes down on the counter and opened them. 'My dad has sent supplies for your sewing bee night. What a fiasco with the sewing shop sneak.' He shook his head and then smiled at Iona. 'I hear he caught you peeking through his letterbox, Iona.'

Iona blinked. She'd never met Gairn, or even heard of him, yet here he was talking to her as if he knew her. But that was fine, she thought, as he was the type of man she felt immediately at ease with. Probably it was his warm smile and his willingness to ply them with cakes.

'A chocolate temptation,' he announced, referring to the large chocolate fudge cake that was topped with dark chocolate buttercream icing. 'And a strawberry and cream sponge cake.' This one was a vanilla cake piped with whipped cream and fresh strawberries.

'Oh, that's so kind of your father,' Jinette told him.

'He thought it would fuel you all up.'

Iona eyed the chocolate cake swithering whether she'd opt for a slice of this or the strawberry and cream sponge. 'These are both far too tempting.'

'Did you make them?' Jinette asked him.

'My dad made the strawberry and cream. I made the chocolate one. I'm intending to specialise in chocolatier work. We'd hoped to take on the empty shop next to our bakery and reopen it as the sweetie shop and as an extension of the bakery.' He shrugged in disappointment. 'But then we heard that it had been inherited, and now of course it's going to be a sewing shop.' His lovely blue eyes looked at Jinette. 'It'll cause nothing but trouble.'

Jinette nodded. 'Well, thank you for bringing us the cakes. They'll go down a treat tonight. And it was lovely seeing you again, Gairn. Don't be a stranger.'

'You too, Jinette, and I'll pop over for a cuppa soon.' He smiled at Iona. 'Nice meeting you, Iona.'

She smiled back at him. 'Nice meeting you too.'

And then he left.

'He's a nice young man, isn't he?' Jinette remarked, carrying the cakes through to the kitchen.

'He is,' Airlie agreed, and then glanced at Iona. 'You and Gairn would make a fine couple.'

Iona held her hands up. 'No, oh no, I'm only here for the summer to relax and enjoying working in the quilt shop.'

'I was trying to nudge her towards Kier,' Jinette called through to them.

Iona shook her head. 'I've put romance on the back burner.'

Airlie smiled at her. 'Maybe better to keep your options open, especially when it comes to romance. Things can hot up nicely during the summer here, even if it's sizzling away on the back burner.'

Iona laughed. 'You're a pair of meddling matchmakers. What hope do I have of behaving myself while I'm here?'

Jinette called through from the kitchen and laughed. 'None at all, Iona.'

CHAPTER THREE

'Parcel for you, Iona.' The delivery driver smiled as he handed her the parcel at the front door of the quilt shop.

Iona smiled, trying not to be taken aback that everyone seemed to know her name. Obviously, he'd seen the update that Jinette had put on the website, welcoming her to the quilt shop. Or she was being gossiped about. Probably the latter.

'Thank you,' Iona said, accepting the parcel and then waved off the cheery courier.

'That will be our embroidery kit packaging,' Jinette said, while sitting behind the counter stitching a quilt.

Iona opened the parcel and confirmed that's what it was. 'Do you want me to start assembling some of the new embroidery kits?'

'If you don't mind. It would let me finish this quilt. The embroidery patterns are in the drawer. Start with the forget–me–nots. We've had orders for those online. We could get them posted today.'

Iona began assembling the kits, adding the pattern, stitching instructions, lovely cotton and linen fabric, and the thread needed to sew the embroidery. She smiled at Jinette. 'This shop is just too tempting. I want this kit. I love these flowers and my fingers are itching to have a go at it.'

Jinette held up her hands. 'That's exactly what happens to me. It's as if my fingers insist I need to start sewing things even when I have lots of other projects on the go. But there is something that always helps me.'

'What's that?' Iona asked, efficiently making up the kits and setting them aside for delivery.

'Tea and cake.' Jinette tried not to smile and continued hand sewing the binding on the quilt.

'I'll put the kettle on. Do you want me to run over to the bakers and get a couple of fairy cakes?'

'I was thinking maybe a slice of chocolate cake or strawberry and cream sponge.'

Iona smiled at her. 'Should we? I mean, the cakes are for the sewing bee night.'

'It's afternoon, near enough, eh? Afternoon tea and a wee wedge of cake would fill the gap nicely until dinner. Though dinner is usually just a quick run round the table for me on sewing bee nights. Once I've finished here, dropped off any extra orders to the post office on my way home, there's barely time for a snatched sandwich before I have to come back.'

Iona nodded and went through to the kitchen and put the kettle on to boil. 'I didn't know we'd be plied with cakes from the bakery. I bought a bag of flour, fresh cream and a bottle of lemonade from the grocers. I was planning to bake lemonade scones — my contribution to the cakes for the sewing bee. You said the ladies usually come armed with cakes and tasty treats.'

'Lemonade scones? Oh yes, make those, Iona. I haven't had them in a while. I've barely time for baking anything.'

'I'll bake the lemonade scones after I've packed the embroidery kits. The recipe is easy, and it'll make me feel like I've made up the deficit for the two slices of cake we've snaffled.'

'Are you into baking?' Jinette asked.

'I enjoy baking. I find it relaxing. But I'm no expert. My cakes and scones aren't elaborate. Nothing like the cakes from the bakery.' Iona set two plates up and looked at the cakes. 'What one would you like?' she called through to Jinette.

Jinette swithered. 'What one do you fancy? And I don't mean Kier or Gairn.'

Iona peered round the kitchen doorway at her. 'You're going to get me into trouble.'

Jinette laughed. 'At least you won't have to ogle Aran in the mornings. I assume he's off your admiration list.'

'He is, not that I have a list, but if I did, his name would have a red line through it.'

'I think you'll still be on his list,' Jinette remarked.

'I doubt that.'

'I saw the way he looked at you. Sometimes men are attracted to women with a wee bit of a wild streak in them.'

Iona made an executive decision and cut into the chocolate cake. It smelled so rich and delicious. She carried the slices through and put them on the counter.

'I wouldn't say that peering through his letterbox qualifies me as wild,' Iona stated.

'You had the nerve to do it.'

'Yes, but you encouraged me.'

Jinette smirked. 'Maybe I am a bad influence after all.'

Iona indicated at the slices of cake with her fork. 'There's no maybe about it.'

They giggled and then tucked into their cake.

After closing the shop for the day, Jinette hurried home to her cottage up the road, and Iona made the lemonade scones.

It was a warm summer evening and Iona sat outside in the quilt shop's garden sipping a glass of refreshing lemonade while the scones baked in the oven.

She loved the vintage style kitchen. It had modern appliances, but everything from the tea caddy to the biscuit tins were vintage finds. If she ever owned a house of her own, she'd definitely scour around for treasures like these to add to her kitchen. Even the ceramic baking bowls and teapots were from a bygone era.

She sighed and relaxed, sitting on a comfy garden chair on the lawn. She sipped her lemonade that still had plenty of fizz in it and enjoyed the fresh air and calm atmosphere. Slipping her shoes off, she felt the cool grass on her bare feet. This was the life, she told herself, the life she dreamed of.

Wisteria adorned the back wall of the cottage and made her long to own a home like this. Sweet peas, fuchsia and other flowers grew along the fence at the bottom of the garden, along with rambling roses. The high fence provided privacy as did the two apple trees in the garden. The fading sunlight flickered through the leaves, and she closed her eyes to unwind in the stillness.

'Hello there, Iona,' a man's voice called out, disturbing the calm.

She jolted and glanced around, wondering where the voice was coming from. And then she saw Aran peering over the garden fence at her. He must've ventured round to the back of the quilt shop.

'Aran!' she called out, astonished to see him. 'What are you doing?' The fence was higher than six feet, so he had to be standing on something to peer over at her.

'Sorry, I didn't mean to startle you. I knocked at the front door, but got no answer. I knew you were in, so I figured you'd be in the kitchen or the garden.'

Her heart thundered from shock and the barefaced cheek of him. Did he really think it was okay to intrude on her privacy?

'What do you want?' she asked him bluntly.

'I wanted to have a quick chat with you. I don't want us to be at loggerheads. The last thing we need is to be fighting against each other in business.'

'So, you're quitting the sewing shop idea and making it into its original sweetie shop?' Her tone was droll.

He smirked, and her heart jolted again, this time due to the sexy grin he threw over the fence at her. 'Very funny, Iona. But no, I had another suggestion.'

She spread her arms and shrugged. 'Speak up. I have scones baking and they're nearly ready to come out of the oven.'

He sniffed the air. With the kitchen door wide open, the scent of home baking wafted out into the garden. 'They smell delicious. There's nothing like home baking on a warm summer night.'

'Nothing quite like a few minutes relaxation and privacy either,' she retorted.

'I'm sorry again, Iona. A hundred apologises in advance.'

'A hundred? Are you planning to make a habit of this? Or doing other sneaky stuff?'

He took the remarks on the chin and didn't retaliate. 'Can I talk to you? Please, just hear me out.'

The timer on the oven pinged. They both heard it.

'Time's up. I have to go. Maybe another time.' She took herself and the remains of her lemonade into the kitchen and closed the door.

The scones had risen nicely and smelled wonderful. She put them on a rack to cool while she hurried through to peer at Aran from the shop window. Yes, there he was heading away, carrying a small step ladder, probably one he used to reach the high shelves to stack fabric.

As if sensing she was watching him, he glanced over his shoulder.

Iona jumped back and nudged one of the rolls of fabric in the window display. She managed to catch it before it knocked everything down like a domino effect.

Aran smiled to himself. He'd seen her reaction. His heart beat faster than he'd felt in a long time when he'd looked at any woman.

23

There was something about Iona that set his senses alight. For the second time that day he envied Kier.

The sewing bee night was busy. Jinette propped the front door of the shop open and members had spilled outside, setting their chairs up in the open air. Most of them were sewing — working on quilts, or stitching home decor items such as cushions, and a few of them were making clothes, especially dresses and skirts.

Knitters were also welcome at the sewing bee, and seeing the shop's lovely new range of local, hand–dyed yarn being used, made Iona want to do some knitting. But there was never enough time to do everything, so she settled down to start piecing her new patchwork quilt from one of the fabric bundles.

Tea, chatter and sewing buzzed around Iona as she told the ladies about Aran.

'He was looking over the fence at you?' one of the ladies asked.

'Yes. He'd even brought a small step ladder with him so he could peer over it,' said Iona.

'He's got a cheek on him,' another lady remarked while stitching hexies for a quilt.

'Aran's a sneaky one,' Jinette said, handing out off–cuts of fabric to the members for their quilting. She always kept any spare pieces of fabric from the shop to use for the sewing bee nights.

'I had the feeling he only wanted to smooth things over to make himself feel better, less guilty about opening a sewing shop,' Iona told them.

Jinette nodded. 'If he'd wanted to be friendly with us, he'd have made his intentions known before things boiled over into a standoff like the one we had this morning.'

'When does he open his new shop?' one of the ladies asked.

'Tomorrow,' said Iona.

'That'll be why he wanted to sweet talk you into easing his conscience,' Jinette said to Iona.

Airlie screwed up her nose. 'I've had a gander at the quilts he's got listed for sale on his website. They're not for me. I don't think he's got a great eye for colour. I'm not just saying that because of what he's done. Though I wouldn't buy anything from him after what he's done to you, Jinette.'

Jinette smiled at Airlie.

'He'll have to make an effort to make things right before I'll go near his shop,' one of the ladies stated.

Jinette sighed. 'I genuinely don't want to be fighting it out with him every day. But I'm not going to let him come here and steal our trade. That's just not on.'

'We're your backup,' Hessie told Jinette. She was a quilter, in her fifties, and a long–time friend of Jinette. Hessie worked from home, but made quilts and other items for the quilt shop, as did most of the other ladies.

'Yes,' Airlie agreed. 'He'd better change his attitude, and his stock, or he'll have us wrangling with him. And he won't like that.'

Jinette sighed again. 'I don't know how we can come to some sort of workable agreement. He's selling items that directly clash with us.'

'Except for the embroidery kits, the yarn, and a better taste in quilts and fabric,' Iona added.

Jinette smiled at her.

'I see you're featuring quilt embroidery on your website, Jinette,' said Milla. She owned the clothes shop that was part of the village post office. Milla was an expert quilter and dressmaker.

'I am. Something again a wee bit different from Aran's quilts.'

'Jinette showed me how to embroider leaves on to on a quilt.' Iona held up the quilt to show them. 'It's a lovely technique. I'm hooked on it now.'

'I'd love to have a go at that,' said one of the ladies. 'Would you show me how you worked the stitches through the quilt layers?'

Iona nodded. 'Yes, I'd be happy to.'

Several ladies tried their hand at quilt embroidery with both Iona and Jinette showing them the techniques and tips they used.

Iona also made a start on embroidering cherry blossom from one of the embroidery kits to help improve her satin stitching.

One of the ladies offered to make more tea.

'We'll have our cake with it,' said Jinette. 'Gairn brought two lovely cakes over for us from the bakers.'

'I can recommend the chocolate cake,' Iona said, smiling.

The ladies laughed.

'But I've made lemonade scones for us,' Iona added. 'Anyone want one?'

A few heads nodded enthusiastically.

'Are you a baker as well as a quilter, Iona?' Milla asked her.

'Just a hobby baker. Scones are easy to make.'

Airlie suddenly noticed Aran when she glanced out the shop window. 'Aran's standing in his window display. He's got the lights on full and he's all lit up while he's working. I think he's trying to get our attention.'

Jinette looked annoyed. 'He could dance a jig in his window wearing nothing but a smile and I wouldn't give him a second glance.'

'Speaking of men who are willing to dance naked, here comes your Lochty,' Airlie told Jinette.

Jinette pursed her lips and shook her head. 'He knows this is our sewing bee night. What's he wanting?'

'He's all spruced up,' Iona remarked.

'And he's trimmed his beard,' Airlie added.

Lochty smiled nervously as he came into the shop.

'You're looking dapper tonight, Lochty,' Hessie told him.

'I had to go to the big town today on business,' he explained. 'I wanted to look less like myself.'

They knew what he meant.

'We're all suitably impressed,' Jinette told him. 'But we're busy having our sewing bee.'

'I know, I know...but...I need to talk to the ladies for five minutes,' he insisted. 'Without you hearing what I'm talking about.'

Jinette frowned. 'What's going on?' Then it dawned on her. 'Does this have something to do with my birthday next week?'

Lochty hesitated. 'Eh, yes it does. So if you could hide in the kitchen for a few minutes that would be handy.'

Jinette smiled, convinced he'd something special planned for her birthday, and headed into the kitchen.

'No listening in, Jinette,' Lochty told her.

'I won't. I like birthday surprises,' she assured him.

He knew this was true and as soon as she closed the kitchen door he faced the ladies with an anxious, wide eyed look.

'What's the matter, Lochty?' Iona asked him.

'It's got nothing to do with her birthday,' he confessed.

'So what is it you want to tell us?' said Airlie.

He looked extra nervous and then took a deep breath. 'I'm going to ask Jinette to marry me.'

There was a stunned silence for a moment and then smiles all round.

'I know I'm going to get a knock back,' he said quickly. 'But I have a plan, something that will give me some wiggle room to make our relationship more...permanent.'

Iona frowned at him. 'What's your plan?'

'When she says no, and she will, I'm going to ask her to get engaged to me.'

'Isn't that the same thing?' said Iona.

'Not quite. If she agrees to marry me, then she'll think we'll have to set a date for the wedding, become my wife, and I think that'll ensure a firm no. So, I'm hoping she'll want to get engaged. We could be engaged for years, forever, if she's not willing to go all the way and walk down the aisle with me.' He dug into his jacket pocket and produced a small blue velvet box. He opened it to reveal a beautiful light sapphire and diamond engagement ring. 'I thought this would help encourage her. I got it at the jewellery shop in the town. I'd ordered it to be specially made for her. What do you think?'

'That's a dazzler!' said Hessie.

Iona gasped. 'Wow! Just wow!'

'What a whopper you've got, Lochty.'

'Thank you, Airlie.'

'Did you pick this yourself?' Iona asked him.

'I did. I know Jinette's tastes, and I wanted to pull out all the stops and really go for it,' he explained.

'If Jinette says no, I'll have it,' one of the ladies joked.

Everyone laughed.

Lochty was concerned about the time. 'I wanted to see what you thought of my idea before I make a numpty of myself. You know Jinette well. Do you think she'll want to get engaged?' He held the ring up and it sparkled with turquoise and diamond light in a band of gold.

The ladies looked at each other for a moment and then nodded and smiled.

'Go for it, Lochty,' Iona encouraged him.

An enthusiastic cheer was all the encouragement he needed. 'Thanks, ladies.' Then he shouted through to Jinette. 'You can come through now, Ettie. I'm away. I'll see you later.'

Jinette didn't hear him. She'd deliberately stepped outside into the garden so she wouldn't overhear or be tempted to listen in.

Iona ran through and opened the kitchen door. 'It's okay now. Lochty's gone.'

Jinette came in from the garden and went through to the shop. She saw Lochty heading away. 'Has he got me something nice for my birthday?'

The ladies smiled and nodded.

Jinette giggled. 'I wonder what it is? I've been hinting I'd like a new overlocking machine for my dressmaking. Is that what he needed your advice for?' Then she immediately held up her hands. 'No, don't tell me. I love surprises.'

Iona exchanged a knowing look with the ladies. Jinette was in for the surprise of her life.

To avoid suspicion, the ladies then steered the conversation back to their sewing.

Lochty glared in the sewing shop window as he walked past on his way to Jinette's cottage. Under other circumstances he'd have stopped and had words with Aran, but he didn't want to spoil what was hopefully going to be one of the happiest nights of his life.

Aran was busy arranging fabric and quilts in his display. He caught the daggered look from Lochty but pretended he hadn't noticed.

Further along the main street Kier was sitting in his car waiting for Lochty.

Kier got out of the car when he saw Lochty approaching.

'We're on,' Lochty announced, sounding excited. 'Thanks for helping me, Kier.'

Kier smiled and lifted a large bunch of flowers out of the car and handed them to Lochty. 'You take these. I'll bring the rose petals and twinkle lights in.'

Lochty nodded enthusiastically and headed into Jinette's cottage. He didn't have a key, but recently, on sewing bee nights, she left the front door open so that Lochty could go in and wait for her coming home. Often he prepared a tasty supper for the two of them. It made him feel like they were one step closer to being a real couple. But tonight he had more planned than just a cup of tea and cheesy toast.

CHAPTER FOUR

Jinette's phone rang while she was chatting and stitching a quilt at the sewing bee. She took the call, thinking that at this time of night it would be Lochty, but she was surprised when she checked the caller's name on her phone.

'Kier! Is there something wrong?' Jinette asked him.

'No, I wondered if I could talk to Iona for a minute. I don't have her number.'

Jinette smiled broadly, sensing a romance was brewing, and called over to Iona who was sitting amid the ladies hand piecing her new patchwork quilt. 'Iona, Kier wants to speak to you.'

The chatter in the bee stopped instantly on hearing that Kier was phoning Iona.

As Iona put her quilting down and headed over, Jinette commented to Kier. 'I hope you're planning to take her for lunch up at the loch tomorrow. She was fair disappointed that your lunch date was just a ruse to scupper Aran.'

'Jinette!' Iona scolded her. She shook her head adamantly.

Kier took in every word, and smiled to himself.

Iona was still blushing and glaring at Jinette as she took the call. 'Hello, Kier.'

'Can Jinette hear me?' he whispered urgently.

Iona casually walked away towards the embroidery thread display. 'No,' she said lightly. The women were listening to every word and she smiled while her heart was pounding wondering what was wrong.

'Lochty forgot to ask you a favour,' Kier relayed quickly. 'Could you and the ladies ensure that Jinette goes home as soon as the sewing bee night is finished. He says she often stays to chat or tidy things up. He needs her to come home soon. He's all set to propose to her tonight.'

'Yes, okay,' Iona said, smiling, pretending to have a pleasant chat with Kier.

Jinette nudged Hessie, indicating that she assumed he'd asked Iona out on a date.

'Is Jinette suspicious?' he whispered.

Iona glanced at Jinette and smiled. 'Not at all.'

'Great. I'll tell Lochty. I'm helping him set up the flowers, twinkle lights and scatter rose petals in the living room of her cottage.'

'That's very nice of you.'

'I'm parked up the road from the quilt shop. I'll give you my number if you need to call me.'

They exchanged phone numbers.

'Can I speak to Jinette again?' he asked.

'Yes, and thanks for calling.' Iona handed the phone back to Jinette.

'I hope you won't mind if I take Iona up to the loch for lunch tomorrow,' Kier said to her. 'If you're not too busy at the shop.'

'Never too busy when it comes to romance, Kier.' Jinette sounded chirpy and smiled at Iona as she finished the call.

Jinette beamed with delight as she announced to the ladies. 'So, we've got a wee romance in our midst.'

Iona shook her head and smiled. 'No, Kier was just phoning me about—'

'Asking you to have lunch with him at the loch,' Jinette cut–in.

Iona kept her smile pasted firmly while being jolted with news of the date.

'Ooh! Lunch with Kier,' Airlie said, smiling at Iona. 'Very romantic.'

Iona realised that Kier had now set a date for them to have lunch. She had no choice but to go along with it so as not to spoil Jinette's surprise proposal night.

'It's just lunch,' Iona said lightly, while feeling the excitement building in her as she realised she did now have a lunch date with Kier. Didn't she?

'I knew he liked you,' Jinette told Iona. 'Promise to tell us all the details.'

'I bet he's a great kisser,' said Milla.

The ladies agreed, causing Iona to blush.

'Oh, look, she's blushing,' Jinette said, smiling at her.

Iona felt the colour rise in her cheeks. 'No wonder. You've made a friendly offer of a bridie and a cuppa into a hot summer fling.'

The ladies laughed.

Iona started to giggle too. She shook her head. 'You lot are incorrigible.'

'I told you that you'd need to pace yourself,' Jinette reminded Iona. 'Bee nights aren't just for sewing. We get up to all sorts of mischief.'

Iona shared a knowing look with the other ladies. 'Maybe you should've been the one to pace yourself, Jinette.'

Jinette checked the time. The evening was wearing on and it would soon be time to start packing their stitching away. 'Yes, it's been a fun wee evening,' she admitted.

Iona smiled as she said, 'And the night is still young.'

'We'll help you clear everything up tonight,' Airlie told Jinette as the bee night came to an end.

Iona had confided to the ladies about Lochty's plan to propose to Jinette at her cottage.

Jinette was gathering up the tea cups and empty cake plates while Iona folded fabric samples and tidied up the shelves.

'I'm fine to clear these dishes away,' Jinette said, not suspecting anything was planned.

Hessie relieved Jinette of the cups and plates. 'Away you go home. We'll sort the shop. You're looking a wee bitty tired. And no wonder. It's been a hard day dealing with Aran and his new sewing shop.'

Airlie and a couple of other ladies ushered Jinette towards the front door.

'Go home and put your feet up, Jinette,' Airlie advised her. 'Iona has keys to lock up.'

Jinette was touched by their thoughtfulness. 'That's awfy kind of you all.' She picked up her sewing bag and hooked it on to her arm. 'It has been a busy day, so tonight I'll take you up on your offer to clear up. Thanks, ladies. See you in the morning, Iona.'

Jinette headed away and they waved her off.

'Phew!' Iona said, sighing. 'I didn't think she was going to leave us to it.'

Milla giggled with excitement. 'I hope Lochty doesn't chicken out from asking Jinette to marry him.'

'It's been a long time coming,' said Hessie. 'Lochty's always loved Jinette.'

'Kier has helped him with flowers and twinkle lights,' Iona explained. 'So I think he's really going to propose to her.'

Airlie folded and stacked the chairs. 'I like Lochty. He can be a handful at times, but he's always been loyal to Jinette.'

'That's a beautiful ring he's bought for her,' one of the ladies remarked.

Milla nodded. 'I love light blue sapphires and diamonds for engagement rings. Oh, to have a man that loved me and gave me a ring like that.' She sighed. 'But I can only dream.'

'It looked very expensive,' said Hessie. 'But Lochty's not short of a shilling. He's not in Kier's wealthy league, but he does okay for himself, and being a single man, he's probably got a tidy wee nest egg.'

'I've only known them a short time,' Iona told them. 'But they seem well suited.'

'They are,' Hessie confirmed. 'They'd make a fine couple. I think Jinette's just clinging on too strongly to the past.'

'I hope she agrees to get engaged.' Milla sounded excited. 'Then we can plan an engagement party up at the manor.'

This idea sparked enthusiasm throughout the other members.

Iona smiled. 'If she surprises him and agrees to get married, I hope I'm here for the wedding.'

'Well,' Hessie mused, 'if Kier and you kindle a wee romance, maybe you'll stay here for a lot longer than the summer.'

The thought of this made Iona remember that her time at the quilt shop was temporary. She'd settled in so quickly, and felt at ease and welcomed by Jinette as soon as she arrived to work at the quilt shop. It was easy to forget that she was the newcomer. Everyone at the sewing bee made her feel equally welcome, and the instant friendships warmed her heart.

After clearing everything away and tidying up the shop ready for the morning, Iona flicked the shop lights off, leaving only the window display lit up.

The ladies were ready to leave when Airlie hesitated. 'I don't think I can stand the suspense. I'd love to know if Jinette says yes to Lochty.'

'I feel the same,' said Iona. 'But I don't want to phone her in case I interrupt their night.'

'We could shark past Jinette's cottage,' Airlie suggested. 'Maybe we'll see a glimpse of them. If they look happy we can sleep easy knowing she accepted the engagement ring.'

Nodding firmly, Iona and the sewing bee ladies headed up the road.

The lights were on in Jinette's cottage, but her lace net curtains prevented them from seeing what was going on inside.

Kier hissed out the window of his car to Iona. 'Have you got a moment?'

Iona was about to hurry over to him when Lochty came rushing out the front door of the cottage and yelled with excitement.

'I think that answers our question,' Hessie commented.

The ladies laughed and cheered.

Lochty waved over to them. He gave Kier a triumphant thumbs up, and then hurried back into the cottage.

With their question answered, the women filtered into the night, each of them heading home. Most lived nearby.

Iona walked over to Kier's car.

He sat in the driver's seat with the window down.

'So Lochty got a yes,' Iona said to him.

Kier smiled and nodded, then clicked the passenger door open. 'Come in for a minute.'

Iona got into the car.

'I'm sorry if I caused you any embarrassment at the sewing bee,' he apologised.

'I was blushing brighter than the cherry blossom I'd been embroidering.'

Kier smiled at her. 'At least you know where you stand with the ladies.'

'Yes, I was standing right in the middle of them encouraging me to have a hot summer fling with you.' The words were out before she could stop herself. 'No, what I mean is—'

Kier cast her a sexy grin. 'A hot summer fling, eh? And there was me thinking you were all busy quilting and working on your new embroidery patterns.'

Iona was glad the car window was open but wished the night air was cooler. She was burning up with embarrassment.

Kier started to laugh.

'Stop laughing,' she chided him, barely able to stop laughing herself.

'Was that cherry blossom bright pink?' he teased her.

Iona swiped him playfully on the arm.

He pretended to be duly scolded.

Iona took a deep breath and realised that she hadn't had so much fun in ages.

'A penny for your thoughts,' he said to her, trying to read her expression.

'I was just thinking...' she shook her head and refrained from telling him.

'Thinking what?' he encouraged her.

She sighed heavily. 'That it's been so long since I've felt this light–hearted and cheerful.'

His grey eyes took on a soulful look as he studied her, realising her life hadn't been easy or filled with happiness.

'Did someone break your heart in the past?' he asked gently.

She nodded, and swallowed the urge to become quite emotional. 'One or two someones, but never the right man for me.'

'Romance is tricky.'

'Oh, yes.' She glanced over at Jinette's cottage. 'But sometimes there is a happy ending.'

He nodded, and looked at the cottage, the lights glowing in the window.

'That really was very kind of you to help Lochty tonight with the flowers and everything,' she said.

He shrugged his broad shoulders. Sitting next to him in his expensive car, she caught a glimpse of his world for a moment. Clearly, he had wealth, and he was sooo handsome, and yet...he wasn't settled with someone who loved him. He had everything that money could buy, plus emptiness.

'Don't tell the ladies, especially Jinette, because I have a bad reputation to protect, but I'm a bit of a softie when it comes to romance,' he confessed.

'My lips are sealed,' she assured him.

Kier gazed for one hot moment at her smiling lips, and suppressed the urge to kiss her right there and then.

'Well,' she said, 'I'd better get back to the shop. I'm up early. A busy day cutting more fabric bundles, and sorting the new embroidery kits. And quilting.' She clicked the car door open and stepped out.

'And a lunch date with me,' he reminded her.

She smiled at him.

'I'll pick you up at the shop at twelve,' he said.

She nodded. 'I'll see you tomorrow, Kier.'

Then she walked away.

He watched her walk the short distance down to the quilt shop, and the longing he felt for her surprised him. Then he started up the car and drove off.

Iona avoided looking over at Aran's shop. He was still working on his window display and getting his shop ready for his opening day.

Unlocking the shop door, she went inside, aware that Aran was probably watching her. The quilt shop lights were on and the window display had been decimated. The new fabric bundles had been bought by the sewing bee ladies and Iona had snapped up another bundle she wanted for quilting.

She could've flicked the lights off and gone through to get ready for bed, but she decided to work on the display.

The quilt shop and the sewing shop were the only two shops ablaze with lights and activity in the main street.

Iona remembered that there was a traditional patchwork quilt in stock on one of the shelves and she put it in the window. The colours were gorgeous and it had a vintage look to it. Jinette had quilted it by hand herself.

She couldn't wait to hear all about Lochty's proposal, and was so happy for Jinette.

Setting up the cutting table, Iona unrolled more of the new fabric and started cutting it into fat quarter bundles for quilting. The floral prints ranged from ditsy to large scale designs. Each bundle had various prints and colour themes and was tied with ribbon.

She'd almost finished refilling the window when she saw Aran walking over. Her heart sank. She didn't want to deal with him, but reluctantly opened the door as he approached. His shirt sleeves were rolled up, but his waistcoat was fully buttoned and he looked as stylish as ever even after working hard to get his shop ready.

His hazel eyes targeted her and he came right out with it. 'Can we call a truce?'

35

'What did you have in mind?'

He sighed as if he'd exhausted himself thinking how to resolve their differences. 'I'm opening my shop in the morning. I've tried to make my window display different from yours. I see you've added a traditional patchwork quilt. I don't even have one of those in stock.'

'Jinette made it. And I have some good news. Jinette was proposed to this evening. She's engaged to Lochty.'

'I don't think I've met him.'

Iona described him briefly.

'Ah, yes, he was glaring at me earlier.'

'So, in the morning, there's going to be a happy and exciting atmosphere around here. Jinette and Lochty will be celebrating their engagement.'

Aran nodded. 'I'm sure they're a popular couple, whereas I'm not popular at all.'

'You haven't exactly endeared yourself to people here.'

'True, but perhaps we can start to get along. I noticed that you're now including embroidered quilts on your website.'

'We are.'

'I don't have any plans for quilt embroidery. Or embroidery kits. And I don't sell yarn.' He glanced at all the colourful skeins and balls of yarn on the shelves.

'I'll tell Jinette that you don't want to compete against her.'

'Thank you.' He went to walk away and then paused. 'Your sewing bee night was very busy.'

'It was. The ladies enjoy getting together to sew, quilt and knit. I'd never been to a sewing bee before I came here. I think it'll be something else I'll miss when the summer's over and I have to leave.'

'You're leaving?' He sounded surprised and disappointed.

'This is only a temporary job, for the summer, while Jinette's assistant is away on business.'

'What about your boyfriend, Kier?'

Iona shook her head. 'He's not my boyfriend.'

Aran frowned. 'I thought...you seemed so close. I assumed you were dating.'

'No, I'm not dating anyone.' Then she reconsidered. 'But Kier has asked me to have lunch with him. It's not a date, and the ladies are encouraging me to have a summer fling.'

Aran blinked. 'They're trying to matchmake you with Kier?'

Iona shrugged. 'Meddling in others love lives is part of the sewing bee,' she said lightly.

'Just as well I'm not part of it. I'm single, so I suppose I'd be fair game for the ladies meddling.'

'I wouldn't rule it out, not with these ladies.'

'Even if I'm not in their good books?'

'Ah, but you're trying to be. If you smooth things over with Jinette, you could have a whole lot of ladies determined to encourage you to indulge in a summer fling.'

'I'm not a summer fling type.'

'That's what I said to them, but it didn't make any difference. Somehow, they managed to set me up on a lunch date with Kier.'

'I thought it wasn't a date.'

'In their minds it is.'

Aran smiled. 'Does that mean I could ask you out sometime, once I'm in your good books?'

Iona was taken aback. 'I, eh...'

He held up his hands. 'No, don't answer that until I have a chance to show you that I'm not the sneaky type you think I am.'

Iona nodded and felt a rush of warmth across her cheeks.

'I don't mean to embarrass you,' he said.

'I just...it's been quite an exciting day. I think I need to get to bed.'

He smirked.

'To sleep,' she emphasised.

'I'll let you get on then. Perhaps if you'd like, pop over during my opening day. I'll have cupcakes and sweets.'

'Maybe.'

Aran smiled. 'At least it's not a no.'

He started to walk away and then threw a comment back to her. 'For what it's worth, I think it was very daring of you to spy through my letterbox.' He laughed and continued on to his shop.

Iona smiled, and locked the shop door. She flicked the lights off, leaving only a small spotlight shining in the window, and got ready for bed.

Tucked up under the pink patchwork quilt, she gazed out at the night sky, and thought about everything that had happened. Aran's hint of asking her out on a date had taken her by surprise. She had a lot to tell Jinette in the morning.

And she thought about Kier. Her heart squeezed thinking of him, and she was excited about their lunch date. Which wasn't a date type of date. He probably wouldn't have asked her if Jinette hadn't meddled. But sitting in his car, his closeness set her senses alight. For a moment she pictured herself indulging in a hot summer fling with Kier, then pushed the notion aside. She needed to get some sleep. She had a busy day ahead of her.

CHAPTER FIVE

Iona opened the quilt shop early and set the tea up ready to welcome Jinette. She couldn't wait to see her wearing her new engagement ring. Iona had never been engaged, or even close to it, and sometimes she wondered if she'd ever meet the right man to settle down with.

She'd made an extra effort with her makeup to look nice and had washed her hair and dried it smooth and silky. It shone like fiery gold under the shop lights, but she was feeling less feisty this morning and more inclined to be pleasantly excited about the busy day ahead. She wore a pale yellow blouse and slim fitting grey trousers so that she'd be tidy for any celebratory photos of Jinette's engagement, and look presentable for her lunch date with Kier. She'd no idea what the terrain at the loch would be, but if it was anything like the surrounding countryside she'd need sensible shoes to navigate it if Kier decided to show her around. Comfy flats were more her style anyway rather than high heels.

The promise of a warm day was assured and another bright blue sky arched over the village. The quilt shop's front door was propped open and the mild air wafted in as Iona refilled the embroidery thread display. The sewing bee members had purchased skeins and spools of thread for the quilting embroidery and other embroidery patterns. She also topped up the gaps where the floral embroidery kits had been. The forget–me–nots, foxgloves and fuchsia kits had been particularly popular. She'd set aside one of the forget–me–nots kits for her own personal use. Embroidering the quilts had definitely improved her satin stitching, so she figured she could tackle the pattern. And she'd done well with the cherry blossom embroidery.

She then cut up fabric into squares suitable for patchwork quilting. Each bundle had a colour theme ranging from blues and green tones to pastel pinks and neutrals.

As she put the quilting bundles in the window, she noticed that the sewing shop was open for business.

Aran stood outside the front window. His back was towards her as he eyed the fabric, quilts and the dress on display.

39

He'd filled a few of the old–fashioned sweetie jars with colourful buttons, beads and other notions. A small set of the shop's original brass scales were weighing spools of thread. A pink sewing machine matched the colour theme. The pink and white striped canopy shielded the window from direct sunlight and added to the pretty look of the shop. It was obviously a sewing shop, but its sweet shop heritage was evident in the little touches he'd included such as a cake stand brimming with cupcakes, chocolates and sweets.

Perhaps it was the cheerful time she'd had at the sewing bee, and the prospect of an engagement party, but she didn't feel as resentful towards Aran as she had done the previous day.

She watched him set up a sandwich board advertising that he was open and welcomed new customers. Then he went back into his shop.

Gazing out the window she saw Jinette walking down the street. Yes, there was definitely an extra spring in her step. She wore a light blue cardigan with a skirt and blouse, and her voluminous sewing bag, that was invariably full of sewing and patterns, was slung over her shoulder.

Iona ran into the kitchen, clicked the kettle on to boil and then hurried back through to welcome Jinette. But her heart sank when she saw that Aran had waylaid her.

Without hesitation, Iona ran over to save Jinette's happy mood being tainted by Aran. Even though he'd promised to behave himself, she didn't trust his motives, not yet anyway.

However, her worries were unfounded when she heard Jinette thank Aran for the engagement gift he'd given her. A peace offering apparently.

'It's okay, Iona,' Jinette assured her, seeing the wide–eyed look on Iona's face as she skidded to a halt in her rush to intervene. 'Aran's given me a wee minding to celebrate my engagement.'

Iona saw the little posy of silk flowers and the patchwork heart on the card he'd made for her. Jinette's ring sparkled in the early morning sunlight as she held the flowers and card in her hands.

'I wish you all the best, Jinette,' he said. 'I'm truly sorry we got off to such a bad start. Things will be different from now on. You have my word.'

Jinette acknowledged his promise and then showed the gift to Iona. 'My first engagement present. Isn't it lovely?'

'It is,' said Iona, feeling relieved that he hadn't spoiled things. 'The flowers are so pretty.' She looked at Aran. 'I didn't know you stocked them. I've always loved silk flowers.'

'I don't have any in stock,' he explained. 'I made them last night from silk fabric. I do have that in stock for dressmaking.'

'You made these?' Iona studied the craftsmanship. 'They're perfect. You should sell them. I'd certainly buy a posy.'

Aran smiled warmly. 'I used to make silk corsages and boutonnieres. I'll consider including them in my listings.'

Iona was then eager to have a proper look at Jinette's ring in the daylight. 'It's dazzling. What a beautiful ring.'

Jinette gave a girlish giggle. 'I didn't think I'd be getting married again, but when Lochty asked me, and produced this ring, well...'

Iona's eyes widened. 'So you're going all the way then? Getting married? Not just engaged forever?'

Jinette frowned and gave Iona a curious look. 'Yes, Lochty asked me to marry him. I've said yes, and now we're setting a date.'

Iona kept any details that Lochty had revealed about his initial plans and smiled brightly. 'That's wonderful. Now you'll have to make your own wedding dress.'

Jinette reacted, sparking with enthusiasm. 'I know. I've been thinking what to wear. Oh, isn't it exciting?'

'I don't wish to poke my nose in where it's not wanted,' Aran began, 'but I used to specialise in wedding gowns before I concentrated on quilting. If you need any assistance, though I'm sure you don't, I'm right here.'

Jinette viewed Aran in a different light. 'You specialised in wedding dresses?'

'Yes, I trained with some of the best in the business for four years when I first started out. I was going to work in fashion design, and I worked for a fashion house in the city. They made exclusive bridal wear, and I was trained to cut the silks, satin, chiffon and other fabrics. Precision cutting for that type of dress is vital. And I learned to encrust the wedding dresses with crystals and pearl beadwork. I loved it, but then I fell in love with quilting. Now I do both. Mainly the quilting, but the dressmaking side will always be a part of my business.'

'And that includes bridal wear?' Iona asked him.

'Yes, but that's more of a personal service,' he explained. 'I don't list wedding dresses. Only my dresses for daywear.'

One of the dresses was in his shop window. A pink and white daisy print dress that Iona wanted as soon as she saw it. It was the type of dress that could be worn comfortably during the day or accessorised for evenings out. She imagined having dinner in a dress like that, and had to blink out of her wayward thoughts.

'If we're going to be friends now,' Jinette began, 'I may take you up on your offer, especially the crystal work. I've always wanted a fairytale wedding dress. I never thought I would. I got married when I was a young lass and my dress was the best satin I could afford at the time. A lovely dress. But now, given a second chance, I may go for the full dazzle of crystals on the bodice.'

'You'd suit an ivory satin. With your colouring and complexion, it would be perfect,' Aran advised.

'I've hardly slept a wink for thinking about it,' Jinette gushed. 'I wasn't sure if I should wear another colour, a pastel pink or soft aqua, you know, with it being my second time around. But then I thought — I'll do what I want, and a beautiful silver white or rich cream dress just makes my heart sing at the thought of it.'

Iona smiled. Clearly Jinette was still in the throws of excitement, and she couldn't have been happier for her. Despite only knowing Jinette a short time, she was the type of person she felt she'd known for years.

Iona gazed at Jinette's ring as the sun shone on the gems and the gold. She took Jinette's hand and lifted it so she could have a closer look at the diamonds and sapphires. 'It's gorgeous. I love looking at it.'

Jinette moved her hand so that it sparkled in the sunlight. 'I love it.' Then she slipped it off and gave it to Iona. 'Be the first to make a wish on it.'

Iona beamed with delight and slipped the ring on and twirled it three times around her finger while making a wish. Then she gave the ring back to Jinette. 'Thank you.'

'I hope your wish comes true,' Jinette said, smiling at her.

Iona noticed the look in Aran's eyes as if he was thinking deep thoughts as he stood there enjoying the moment.

'I obviously can't tell you what I wished for,' said Iona, 'but if it ever comes true, I'll give you a hint.'

'Did you wish to never run out of quilting fabric?' Jinette joked with her.

Iona shook her head. 'No, I can't tell you, or it won't come true.'

Aran took a guess. 'Is it that you'll meet the love of your life this summer and settle down with him?'

Iona's heart twisted. He was so close to the truth.

At that moment, Gairn came hurrying out of the bakers. The scent of fresh baked bread wafted out with him. 'I heard the news, Jinette. Congratulations!' He gave her a peck on the cheek. 'I'll bring a cake over to you later this morning. I want to ice something special on it.'

'You don't need to go to any bother for me,' Jinette said, while hoping that he would.

'Nonsense. When one of us gets engaged, we all celebrate in this village,' Gairn assured her.

This was the first time that Gairn had come face to face with Aran. But seeing that he'd become friendly with Jinette and Iona, Gairn nodded acknowledgement to his next door shop neighbour.

Aran returned the gesture, wary of saying anything that would tilt the friendly balance he seemed to have achieved.

'So, this is your opening day,' Jinette said, having a look at the sewing shop. The pastel pink exterior looked lovely in the morning light, and Aran had styled his window display using pinks, sky blues and pale greens. She admired the pink sewing machine in the window and his decorative fabric bunting.

Iona reconsidered whether he had a good eye for colour after all. The fabrics looked enticing, as did the dress, and the main quilt he had on display was a patchwork of pink, blue and lilac. She had to admit that his shop looked great.

Aran smiled. 'I don't expect to have many local customers. But that's fine because I've had plenty of online orders, so I'll be kept busy stitching quilts for my customers.'

'I hope you can keep up with demand,' Jinette commented. 'I'm lucky that several of the sewing bee ladies also help make the quilts we sell in the shop. And I have Iona to help me.'

'That's the chance I'm taking with this shop,' Aran admitted. Then he gestured to them. 'Would you like to come in for a quick look?'

He was inviting Iona and Jinette, but Gairn included himself and went in with them.

'The shop still has a scent of vanilla and sweets,' Jinette said, sniffing the air and smiling.

'It smells delicious,' Iona added. 'It must've been a very pretty sweet shop in its day.'

'I remember it being pink and cream,' Gairn recalled.

'It was,' said Aran, 'but I painted the whole interior a warm white so the colours of the fabric can be viewed clearly.'

Jinette gazed around, seeing all the fabric on the shelves and displays. 'I used to love their home made sweets as well as their regular range. The village could do with a lovely wee sweetie shop, but you've certainly made it look great with all these beautiful fabrics.' She went over to his selection of cottons.

'I'll try not to clash with your quilt shop,' Aran promised. 'These are a new line of quilting weight cotton fabrics that I'm hoping will be popular.'

Gairn wandered around, out of his depths when it came to sewing and quilting, but he admired what Aran had done with the shop. 'I don't know anything about fabric, but even I think these look nice.'

'Do you sell any fancy sweets, like chocolate truffles, in your bakery?' Aran asked Gairn.

'You're in luck. I made a whole selection of them last night,' Gairn said to him.

'Gairn is training to be a master baker and chocolatier,' Jinette told Aran.

'I've put a cake stand in the window with slices of cake, cupcakes and chocolates,' said Aran. 'But I want to fill this cake stand on the counter with lots of fancy chocolates and truffles. I'll buy a selection from your bakery. I want to offer anyone coming in a sweet while they're browsing.'

'Chocolate fingers and pristine fabrics aren't always a good mix,' Gairn warned him.

Aran glanced at Iona and Jinette. 'What would you advise? You serve tea and cake at the sewing bee. Is there an issue with sticky fingers?'

Jinette shook her head. 'No, the ladies are careful not to mess up the fabric while they're having their tea and cake. But customers may not be quite so mindful.'

'I'll give you a selection of the sweets that are in foil or wrappers,' Gairn suggested. 'They're less messy.'

Aran nodded firmly. 'I'll take whatever you can offer.'

Leaving them to it, Gairn went back to the bakery to get the sweets.

'Could I ask a favour of you, Iona?' said Aran. 'When you see Kier for lunch today, could you ask him if he would supply me with flowers for hanging baskets for the front of my shop. Probably a small ornamental flowering tree as well.'

'Yes, I'll ask him and let you know,' said Iona.

Aran nodded his thanks. 'Okay, so have you time for a quick look at my new patterns or are you hurrying off to start your day of celebrations?'

Jinette exchanged a look with Iona. 'I think we've time for a wee peek at what you have on offer.'

Iona thought Aran looked particularly classy in his cream collarless shirt worn with a waistcoat. But her heart didn't react the same as when she'd looked at him before she found out he was opening a sewing shop. Perhaps the mistrust had taken the shine off her attraction to him. She supposed this would make it easier to be friendly without fancying him.

They were looking at Aran's quilt patterns when Gairn came hurrying back in with samples of chocolates and bonbons. 'Do you fancy sweets like these?' He held out a plateful of samples. 'Try one of the chocolates.'

Aran picked a gold foil wrapped chocolate. 'Yes, these are perfect. Too perfect in fact. I'm tempted to keep these for myself,' he joked.

Gairn offered the plate of chocolates to Iona and Jinette.

'This is delicious,' Jinette said, enjoying a white chocolate truffle.

Iona sampled one of the dark chocolate covered fudge squares. 'These are too tasty.'

Gairn laughed. 'So you approve then, Iona?'

With a mouthful of melting tasty fudge and chocolate Iona nodded enthusiastically.

Jinette poured through the patterns, taking in the designs and mentally compared them to her own. He seemed to have a liking for geometric patterns, while she preferred other designs.

Iona had now wandered over to the fabric bundles. 'I'm noseying at your fat quarter bundles, Aran.'

'Nosey away,' Aran told her, laughing.

'Is that the silk fabrics you sell up there on that high shelf?' Jinette asked him.

'Yes, I keep them out of reach because the silk and satin marks so easily.' He grabbed the step ladder he'd used to peer over Iona's garden fence, and climbed up to the bolts. 'This ivory white satin has a tiny wedding ring design on the fabric. Perfect for a wedding dress.'

Jinette's face lit up with interest. 'Bring it down. Let me have a look at it. I won't touch it with my chocolate fingers.'

Aran brought the bolt of gorgeous fabric down and unrolled a measure of it to let them see it.

'That's beautiful,' Jinette enthused.

Iona admired at it too. 'Yes, that's one of the loveliest satin prints I've seen.'

'It's an exclusive design. Quite expensive, but I'd happily give you a huge discount if you decided you wanted it for your wedding dress,' Aran offered.

Jinette laughed. 'You're a slick salesman, Aran. But yes, you're on to a winner with me. I've always loved fabric at first glance. And this, yes, I love it. Put the bolt aside for me, and if anyone else wants it, give me first dibs at buying it, discount or no discount.'

'Consider it done,' Aran assured her. 'But don't feel obliged to use this. Take your time. After all, you've only just got engaged. In the throws of all the excitement, you could make a hasty decision. I'd hate to be blamed for strong–arming you into using this for your wedding dress.'

Jinette smiled. 'Thank you, but I think I've seen the fabric I've always dreamed of having. I saw a wedding dress once and it was printed with the faintest wedding bells design, all in white, like this fabric. I wished I'd had the chance to make a dress with it.'

'Now you have,' Iona encouraged her. 'The ivory white satin is gorgeous.'

'Will you be setting a date soon for the wedding?' Gairn asked her.

'Yes. We were talking about it last night and Lochty says that with it being the summer the weather would be sort of guaranteed to be bright and sunny. So I think we'll be aiming for a summer wedding.' She sounded so excited.

Iona smiled, happy for her. A summer wedding certainly outshone a summer fling. Then she remembered that if the wedding was in the late summer she may have left. A pang of sadness swept through her. How easy it was to forget that she was only a temporary assistant and nothing and no one here was going to be part of her future.

Gairn set the chocolates and bonbons on the cake stand, but noticed the sad expression on Iona's lovely face. He stepped close to her while holding the empty plate. 'Are you okay, Iona?' he whispered.

She immediately brightened, realising her innermost thoughts had expressed themselves openly. Jinette and Aran was busy chatting about sewing machines and hadn't noticed. 'Yes, I'm fine,' she lied.

Gairn's lovely blue eyes gave her a knowing look. 'No, you're not fine. What's wrong?'

Iona glanced over to see that Jinette and Aran were still steeped in conversation, and then revealed to Gairn what was wrong. 'I'm only here for a few weeks during the summertime. If Jinette gets married in the late summer, I probably won't even be here. I'll have left.'

Gairn recognised the sadness in her. 'I understand. I'm only here for the summer too, then I'm back in Edinburgh to finish my training.'

Iona nodded, taking in what he was telling her.

Gairn continued to confide in her. 'Every day I'm here, I keep thinking how much I'll miss the bakery and the village when I leave. It's as if everything is tainted with a bit of sadness, like I'm adding it on to everything I do.'

'I've been doing that,' she whispered. 'It takes the happy edge of things.'

Gairn nodded. 'But it's hard not to dwell on leaving when living here is so great. I can't wait to finish my training and come back here to settle permanently. I've been offered the chance to work abroad, or in London, or maybe stay in Edinburgh and find a patisserie position with one of the hotels.' He shook his head adamantly. 'But I don't want that. I want to build my business along with my father at the bakery. The city isn't for me. It never has been. I'm only there to train and qualify, hopefully.'

'I'm sure you will, especially if those chocolates are a sample of what you can make,' she said encouragingly.

'That's very nice of you, Iona.' Then he sighed. 'Is there any way you could stay on at Jinette's shop?'

'No, Eevie's coming back and intends to continue with her old job. It's fair enough, and I knew the position was a temporary one, but...'

'The lifestyle here is great?' he suggested.

Iona nodded enthusiastically. 'It is. I love it. And I love living in the cottage while working at the shop. It's perfect. I won't find that kind of perfect when I go home to the large town that I belong to.'

'Maybe you belong here now?' he whispered.

Jinette glanced round at them. 'What are you two whispering about? Up to mischief no doubt.'

'You have us sussed, Jinette,' Gairn pretended to confess.

Aran felt a pang of envy. Gairn seemed to be getting along well with Iona.

Jinette waved Iona over to where Aran's sewing machine was set up. 'Come and have a look at Aran's sewing machine. It's the same one that I use in my shop, but his is the latest model.'

Iona went over to admire the machine. 'Very nice.'

Jinette sat down at it. 'It's got lots more buttons to press and extra doodahs.'

'What type of sewing machine do you use for your quilting?' Aran asked Iona.

'I'm a hand quilter. I don't machine my quilts,' Iona told him.

Aran frowned. 'What? You hand quilt everything?'

'Yes. I've always loved hand quilting,' Iona explained. 'I have used a machine when someone has specifically asked for that. I sold my quilts from home, online, and if someone expected it to be machined, I'd do it. But my preference is definitely hand quilting.'

'I'm the complete opposite,' said Aran. 'I machine every part of it, including the binding.'

'I use both methods,' Jinette added.

Iona glanced around, realising that Gairn had gone back to his shop, leaving them to chat about their respective sewing and quilting shops.

Gairn selected a large birthday celebration style cake that was covered in white royal icing from the bakery display and set about icing Jinette and Lochty's names on it with two hearts and two rings entwined, indicating their engagement and forthcoming wedding. Gairn's father approved of this and was pleased that his son had the talent to do it.

While working on the cake, Gairn saw Kier walking past the front window. He was out delivering flowers to his customers.

Gairn tapped on the window to gain Kier's attention and beckoned him to come in.

'Iona and Jinette are next door in Aran's shop. It's his opening day. He's sweet talking them into liking him.'

'Is it working?' Kier asked, hoping that Aran didn't lavish too much attention on Iona.

'Oh, yes. They're talking about Aran selling Jinette fabric for her wedding dress, and helping her to make it.'

'Really?'

Gairn nodded. 'He's even got me liking him enough now to supply him with chocolates for his opening day.'

'I'll stay well away then,' Kier said lightly.

Gairn shook his head. 'I'm afraid you're being inveigled to provide flowers for the front of his shop.'

'Am I now?'

'Uh–huh.'

'I guess I'd better make an appearance,' Kier said, sighing.

'I would if I was you, if only to pry Iona and Jinette out of his friendly clutches.'

Kier lowered his voice and said, 'Has Aran made any moves on Iona?'

Gairn felt he should confide what he sensed. 'He looks at Iona like...well, I think he's taken a shine to her, if you know what I mean.'

Kier nodded. He knew exactly what Gairn meant. 'Thanks for the tip–off.'

'Any time.' Gairn then lifted a plate of his chocolate samples and offered it to Kier. 'Try one. It'll take the edge off of any bitter taste of rivalry.'

They laughed, half joking and yet with a hint of earnest concern that Aran was set to make a play for Iona.

Kier popped a chocolate in his mouth and lifted a second. He'd a feeling the rivalry was going to taste very bitter. He was looking forward to his lunch date with Iona. Now he had Aran to contend with. A man with a lot more in common with Iona than he did. He knew next to nothing about quilting and sewing. Flowers, yes, but sewing? He could sew a button on his shirt, but that was a task he rarely enjoyed or had a talent for. Now Aran was on the scene, plying Iona with pretty fabric and discussing patterns and templates or whatever it was that was needed to create the beautiful quilts that Jinette's shop sold.

Running an anxious hand through his thick blond hair, he popped the second sweet into his mouth and ventured into Aran's domain.

'Kier!' Iona chirped, obviously happy to see him.

This bolstered Kier and warmed his heart. Seeing her certainly caused his heart to react. She looked especially lovely this morning. Her hair looked like spun amber under the shop's spotlights.

Iona hurried over to him. 'Aran wants to know if you can supply flowers for the frontage of his shop.'

Kier kept his smile steady. It was genuine towards Iona, and Jinette, but he still kept his guard up against Aran.

Aran smiled tightly. He envied Kier's relationship with Iona. But from what he'd heard, and gossip was plentiful in the village and easily overheard, their rendezvous at the loch was their first date. He didn't want to spoil things for Kier, but if they weren't even a couple yet, just friends with potential, then the gloves were off.

'Yes, what type of flowers did you want?' Kier asked him.

Aran looked at Iona for her advice. 'What do you think would look nice?'

Iona didn't hesitate. 'Lots of small, colourful flowers, ones that trail from hanging baskets. And a gardenia tree. Gardenia flowers are gorgeous.'

'I'll take Iona's advice,' Aran said to Kier. 'Do you think you could provide something like that?'

'Definitely,' Kier assured him, wise to his involving Iona in making the decision.

Iona beamed, delighted that he'd taken her suggestion.

Kier smiled but deep down he knew that was a shrewd move from Aran. He didn't doubt that Aran wanted the flowers, but he sensed he also wanted Iona for himself. He knew he'd have to be ready to ward off Aran's sweet talking ploys, or risk Iona falling for Aran.

CHAPTER SIX

'I want to hear all the details,' Iona said to Jinette when they finally extricated themselves from Aran and went to start work at the quilt shop. 'I believe rose petals and twinkle lights were involved.'

'They were.' Jinette was happy to tell her about the proposal. 'Lochty had scattered rose petals on the carpet in the living room and he'd lit the room with twinkle lights.'

'What did you think when you saw this?' Iona asked excitedly.

'I knew he had something special planned, but I still thought it had to do with my birthday. Maybe an early birthday gift.' Jinette smiled. 'I didn't think for a moment that he was going to propose. But then he told me that he loved me, he'd always loved me and asked me to marry him. He produced the ring and held it out, hoping I'd accept.'

'I'm so glad you did.'

'So am I.' She gazed at the ring on her finger. 'Apologises in advance, Iona. You're going to have to endure me admiring my ring a hundred times a day.'

Iona smiled. 'It's one of the most beautiful engagement rings I've seen. It's my taste. So classy, yet bright and dazzling. It's the type of ring I'd have if I was ever lucky enough to find the right man.'

'I think you will. You're too lovely not to find happiness with a nice man. I know you've picked duds in the past, but you're wiser now. It's just a matter of finding Mr. Right. But maybe you're having lunch with him today?'

Iona's heart thundered at the thought of this. 'I don't know what type of lunch date we'll have. It could be a picnic courtesy of the bakery, admire the view, a tour of the loch's scenery, and then get dropped off back to reality at the shop. Not that I'm unhappy working here.'

'I know what you mean,' Jinette assured her. 'But first dates are exciting. You should enjoy yourself.'

'The thing is, we've not really established that it's a proper date.'

'I doubt that Kier is inviting you just to be friends.'

Iona gave Jinette a chiding look. 'You're the one that encouraged him. If you hadn't prompted him by saying I was disappointed that our supposed date wasn't real, he would never have asked me.'

'Nonsense, Kier likes you. He would've asked you, but he'd have taken his sweet time about it, and perhaps missed his chance. It's obvious that Aran is poised to pounce on you.'

Iona blinked. 'What?'

Jinette clarified her comment. 'If Kier wasn't on the scene, I strongly suspect that Aran would've made a move on you. He'd have asked you to have dinner up at the mansion. Something like that. A proper date. He even looked jealous when Gairn and you were whispering secrets to each other in his shop. A man like Aran doesn't react like that unless he's got a wee fancy for you.'

Iona laughed.

'I'm serious,' Jinette insisted.

'That's why it's so funny.'

Jinette smiled. 'What a wonderful pickle we've got ourselves into, Iona. Yesterday, our main concern was whether to have chocolate cake or strawberry and cream sponge. Now I'm intending to walk down the aisle with Lochty — and you're causing Kier and Aran to fight for your affections.'

'That sounds so dramatic, and yet...'

'It pretty much sums up where we stand.' Jinette took a deep breath and propped the shop door open to let the warm summer air waft in. 'I don't know about you, but I'm too giddy to even think about dealing with the shop orders.'

'I'll check the online sales and pack up what I can. Though no guarantee my mind won't wander to thoughts of Kier.' Iona checked the time. 'Where did the morning go?' She sounded shrill. 'He's picking me up in an hour.'

Jinette listed off exactly where the time had been burned. 'Noseying in Aran's shop. Planning my wedding dress. And you causing ructions with the local totty.'

Iona guffawed.

Jinette continued, 'Eating Gairn's chocolates and causing emotional havoc for ourselves burned half the morning too.'

'That I can agree with.'

'And that's another thing...Gairn's a handsome one too. Could he be the man for you? The two of you seem to have sparked an easy friendship.'

'Don't even start.' Iona smiled and shook her head. 'Gairn is nice, but I don't see us becoming anything other than friends.'

Jinette wasn't convinced. 'We'll see. But it would be nice if Kier finally found someone to settle down with.'

'Despite him having a reputation as the local heartbreaker?'

Jinette swept this notion aside. 'Seeing the way Kier reacts when he's around you makes me reconsider this. I've known him for years, and I can tell that he's attracted to you. He'd make a fine husband.'

'Who would make a fine husband?' Kier asked, taking them aback when he'd come into the shop without them noticing. With the front door propped open, he'd walked in on their conversation without them hearing him.

'Lochty,' Iona said, hiding her embarrassment that they'd been talking about him.

Kier looked at her and smirked. 'I'm beginning to sense when you're telling fibs, Iona.'

Jinette jumped in to defend Iona. 'We'd been talking about Lochty, but I also mentioned that Gairn is fine husband material.'

Kier's confidence took a battering, but he tried to smile. 'Yes, I suppose he is. And more trustworthy than Aran. Though I'm not saying that Aran is sneaky, just not quite as open with his intentions as Gairn.'

Iona tried to change the subject. 'You're early.'

'I'm a bit early,' Kier agreed. 'But I wanted to check what you'd fancy for your lunch. There's always a queue at the bakers near lunchtime, so I thought I'd go a bit early and buy something we can take with us. What would you like?'

'I'm sticking with the bridie,' said Iona. Secretly, her heart squeezed just looking at Kier. He'd clearly showered and changed into a light blue shirt and his jeans enhanced his long, lean, strong build. If anyone was a heartbreaker, he surely was. His pale grey eyes studied her. He seemed to sense when she was telling fibs and could read her quite well. She blushed at the thought that he could sense the effect he had on her just standing there looking so tall, fit and handsome.

'A bride it is,' he said, and then fumbled to correct himself. 'Sorry, I mean a bridie. All this talk of engagements,' he added as an excuse.

Jinette gave Iona a knowing look.

'I've made us a flask of tea,' he said. 'It's in the car. Is there anything else you fancy?'

Apart from kissing him until her breath was ragged, Iona thought wickedly, then chided herself. 'Cake would be nice. Cupcakes, something like that.'

'I'll buy cake as well,' he said. Jeez, he could hardly contain the effect she had on him. There were times when just looking at her sent his senses into a tail spin. When she'd sat next to him in his car the previous night, he'd felt the urge to kiss her, yet protect her. Every time he saw her the feelings were becoming more intense. Maybe all the talk of engagements and marriage was disrupting his usual calm. He wasn't a man to be easily ruffled or affected by being close to a woman he found attractive. But he couldn't remember the last time he'd ever felt so giddy. If she knew even half the effect she had on him, he'd be mortified with embarrassment.

'Do you have a blanket to sit on?' Jinette asked him. 'There's nothing to sit on at the loch.'

Kier sighed. He'd forgotten the blanket. He'd left it on the back of the sofa in his house.

'I can give you one of the quilts we use for the sewing bee,' said Jinette. She went over to the cupboard and pulled one down from a shelf. 'This isn't precious, so don't worry about putting it down on the grass and lying on it.'

Iona's glared at Jinette.

'Sitting on it,' Jinette corrected herself. 'I wasn't suggesting that the pair of you will be rolling around on the grass.'

Iona eye–balled Jinette to stop making things sound worse. She was blushing bright pink.

This was Kier's cue to leave. 'Okay,' he said, trying to sound casual. 'I'll pop over to the bakery and come back in about half an hour.' He took the quilt with him and left.

'That was so embarrassing,' said Iona.

Jinette tried not to laugh.

This made Iona break into a giggle. She shook her head. 'Come on, let's pack some of the online orders.'

They busied themselves packing the orders that included cutting material for the new fabric bundles and selecting thread and yarn.

The orders were piled up on the counter.

'That's a load of orders ready to go,' Jinette announced. She checked the time and smiled at Iona. 'Nearly time for your hot date.'

Iona sighed. 'I'm a bit on edge, especially when you tease me. It's not a *date* date,' she emphasised.

'If I know Kier, it'll be a lot more than a quick smooch and a sausage roll,' Jinette said loudly.

'Sounds like a hot date to me,' Gairn commented, walking in on their conversation. He was carrying a cake box. 'Make room for your cake,' he said, bustling over and forcing Jinette to move a pile of parcels so he could put the box down. He opened the lid to reveal the classic white royal iced cake. He'd written Jinette and Lochty's names entwined with two rings — an engagement ring and a band of gold.

He expected squeals of delight from Jinette, but instead she was silent. He exchanged a worried look with Iona.

Then they noticed that Jinette was so overcome seeing her engagement cake that she was trying not to shed a tear.

'It's beautiful, Gairn,' Jinette said in a slightly shaky voice. 'I'm sorry I'm a wee bit emotional. But I think it's just hit me that I'm engaged. I'm so happy.'

Iona started to sniff, trying to contain her emotions.

Even Gairn felt a wave of emotion wash over him.

Jinette smiled and took a deep breath. 'I can't thank you enough for making such a lovely cake.' She looked at Iona. 'Will you help me take photos before you head off for lunch?'

'Yes.' Iona brought her phone out and the first picture she took was of Jinette standing beside Gairn. He was holding the cake box open at an angle so that the cake could be seen. They both smiled happily.

Iona was snapping pictures when Kier arrived.

'Beautiful cake,' said Kier. 'Don't hurry. Take your time. Get all the photos you need,' he assured Iona.

'Come on,' Jinette said to Kier. 'Get in the picture with us.'

Kier smiled and stood on the opposite side of Jinette.

Iona captured the happy moments, the three of them all genuinely happy.

Kier then went over to Iona. 'Give me your phone and I'll take snaps of you too.'

Iona handed Kier the phone and then stood beside Jinette and Gairn.

Kier clicked plenty of photos of them together, some with just Jinette with her cake, Jinette's hand with the ring and the cake, and then suggested she stand outside her shop.

'Stand in front of the shop with your cake,' said Kier. 'This is one you can put up on your website to tell your customers the engagement news.'

'That's a great idea,' Jinette chirped, happy to go along with his suggestion.

A lot of photos were taken outside, including pictures that Jinette wanted of Iona.

'I want plenty of smiling memories of you being here at the shop,' Jinette said to her.

Iona smiled as she stood in front of the window, but deep down, her heart felt so sad. She would be leaving, and these pictures would be part of the little quilt shop's past. The summer when Iona had been her temporary assistant.

Kier didn't see the secret turmoil in Iona, but Gairn did. He gave her a nod, acknowledging that he understood. A shared moment that helped her keep smiling while the photos were being taken.

Iona then held her phone and was ready to leave with Kier. 'I'll send all of these pictures over to you, Jinette.'

'I'd appreciate that, Iona,' Jinette said, and then nodded and smiled at Kier and Gairn. 'Thanks again to both of you. I hope you'll be coming to my engagement party soon.'

'Wouldn't miss it,' Gairn said firmly.

'Neither would I,' Kier seconded.

'Great,' Jinette said chirpily. 'Okay, I won't keep you two from your lunch date. Have a lovely time. And don't do anything that I would do.'

'Don't you mean what you wouldn't do?' said Iona.

Jinette gave her a cheeky grin. 'I know exactly what I mean.'

Laughing, Iona left the shop with Kier. Gairn walked with them. Kier's car was parked outside the bakers.

A pair of jealous eyes peered out the window of the sewing shop at the three of them. Aran sighed heavily. He hated feeling like a jealous fool, but he couldn't help being attracted to Iona, and wished he was the one having a date with her.

As Kier drove off with Iona, Aran busied himself in the shop. He sat down at his sewing machine and started whirring through the layers of the quilt he was making. By concentrating on his stitching he hoped this would take his mind off Iona.

Kier drove them through the countryside with the windows open. The sun was streaming through the trees and the scent of the flower fields wafted in.

Iona gazed out the window, admiring the scenery. 'The fields look beautiful,' she remarked, not knowing that they belonged to Kier.

He smiled and continued driving.

'What is it? Why are you smiling?'

'Those are my fields.'

'All of these are yours?' She sounded impressed.

He nodded and indicated towards a stylish farmhouse. 'That's my house.'

Iona looked at the lovely white farmhouse set in the large estate. A narrow road led off the main road they were driving along.

'You're welcome to come and view the fields sometime,' he offered casually.

'I'd like that. I love flowers. Do you tend the fields yourself?'

'I work the fields on the entire estate, but I have people to help me, especially during the busy seasons — spring and summer. Lochty's helping me during the summertime along with several other workers.'

Iona thought about the things Jinette had mentioned about Kier, including how rich and successful he was.

He saw the look on her face. He'd seen that look before, so he decided to explain about his wealth. 'I'm fortunate to have inherited money, and I have other investments that enable me to subsidise my fields if there's a lean season. Luckily, the weather here is ideal for growing flowers.'

Iona felt the heat of the sun shining through the open window. 'It feels like the height of summer even though it's barely the end of the spring.'

'We're inland, so there's no cold coming in from the coast, and we're in a sheltered basin in this area of the Highlands, protected by the rolling hills and lush landscape.'

She sighed and breathed in the fresh, fragrant air. It smelled of jasmine and roses and greenery. 'It's so refreshing.'

'The seasons are strong but overlap. The spring arrives early and lingers into the early summer.'

'Yes, there's still pink blossom on the trees in the main street,' Iona commented.

He nodded. 'The summers are long, and the autumn trails well into the winter months. This makes the winter quite short. We have plenty of snow, and white Christmases are guaranteed. But the winters aren't long.'

'That's handy, especially for your type of work. I suppose the fields are quite bare in the heart of the winter.'

'They have a stark beauty. Despite the cold, I grow winter hardy varieties of flowers — heather, hellebores, winter jasmine, wintergreens with red berries, shrubs and evergreens. The trees help to protect the fields during the winter. I have blue spruce, silver firs, winter cherry — they look ethereal when they're covered in snow.' He looked thoughtful. 'I love the spring and summer, and the autumn, but the season that I love the most is the winter.'

'I've always loved the winter and the summer. Frosty days and hot summer nights. I suppose I love extremes.'

'Then you'd love the winters here. It's a pity you're leaving after the summertime.'

Iona felt a stab of disappointment. 'I seem to keep missing out. I'm often leaving places when I'd rather stay, and going back to places I'd rather have left behind.'

'That sounds complicated.'

She nodded.

'Is there any chance you could change that pattern?' he said. 'Stay where you want to be, and don't go back to whatever you wanted to leave behind.'

'I wish I could, but usually things don't work out that way. Take this summer for instance. Here I am, but I know I'll have to go home in several weeks time.'

Kier bit his lips, and she noticed how sexy he looked when he did this. Again, she was tempted to kiss him even though she would never be so bold.

'Are there things you need to sort out back home? You live in a large town?'

'I do. I share a flat with other women, and they're expecting me to go home when this temporary job is finished.'

'Jinette could ask you to stay.'

'No, it was always clear that I'm standing in for Eevie, and she's coming back to work as Jinette's assistant and live in the cottage.'

'What are your plans after leaving here?' he asked.

She sounded vague. 'Look for another job, sewing, quilting work. I'd like to be able to make a living from selling my quilts or working for a shop like the quilt shop. And I'd love to own my own shop.'

'Any plans to settle down?'

'That's a complicated answer.'

'Tell me. I'm listening.' He continued to drive through the countryside while she explained.

'I'd like to settle down, but still sew my quilts. The issue isn't the quilting, it's dating the wrong men. Not that I'm a serial dater. I'm not, but I have a tendency to pick the wrong men. I have a knack for it.'

He smiled, and yet his heart ached. That feeling of wanting to protect her washed over him again.

She forced herself to brighten up. 'But Jinette says that the man for me could be right around the corner.'

Or sitting next to you, Kier thought.

Iona pointed out the window. 'Oh, look. There's the loch. Isn't it?'

'It is. Not far now.' He took a turnoff down a road that narrowed up to the loch. Heather in tones of lilac, white and pink carpeted the area, along with green fields and a lush rolling countryside backdrop.

Kier drove them along and parked the car facing the loch.

Iona smiled and gazed out at the view. The water reflected the surrounding countryside, and it seemed as if they had it all to themselves. No other cars were nearby, and no one else was around.

'Is it usually so quiet here?' she asked.

He nodded. 'It becomes busier in the heart of the summer, especially with tourists, or during the summer fayre. But most times, it's calm and quiet.'

Iona felt excited and stepped out of the car on to the grass. She looked around. A blue sky arched over the landscape and sunlight sparkled on the surface of the loch. Long grass edged the loch, and it was so calm and quiet that she could hear the gentle buzz of the bees enjoying the wildflowers nearby.

Kier joined her.

She kept forgetting how tall he was, towering over her, as he stood beside her gazing out over the loch.

'The air is so clear and fresh,' she said, taking a deep breath, feeling the benefit of it.

'I've been coming here since I was a boy. I still come here regularly when I want to clear my head, sort out my thoughts.'

She pictured him as a boy, running around, all blond hair and mischief. 'It must've been a wonderful place to grow up.'

'It was. I used to run up those hills and then roll down over and over until I reached the bottom. I'm exhausted even thinking about it now. But then I'd fall asleep on the heather beds.'

'Heather beds?'

'Yes.' He motioned towards a banking of heather nearby. 'Come on, try it before we have our lunch.' He clasped her hand and hurriedly led her over to an area of lilac coloured heather.

Iona giggled as she let him lead her. 'What are you doing?'

'Lie down,' he said, letting go of her hand and pointing at the thick blanket of heather. 'Try it, come on.' He lay down on it to show her what he meant.

'Okay,' she said, and lay down too. Whatever she was expecting, she was wrong. It was so soft and comfortable. 'Oh. My. Goodness.'

Kier laughed lightly. 'Isn't it perfect bedding?'

'You start lunch, I'll just lie here,' she joked.

He tipped his head to gaze at her and his smile seemed boyish. 'It has just the right amount of springiness, and the scent of the heather is like aromatherapy of sorts. But it's so comfortable.'

Iona didn't say anything.

'What do you think?' he prompted her.

She still didn't reply, and pretended to have fallen asleep.

He smiled, getting the joke, and nudged her awake.

She laughed and enjoyed the moment of closeness and shared smiles.

He finally stood up and grabbed her hand. 'Come on sleepy head. Time for lunch. Unless your bridie has my name on it?'

She jumped up, still holding his hand, and they raced back over to the car.

Kier brought the picnic food out and peeked into one of the bakery's paper bags. 'These bridies smell delicious, and they've still got some heat in them.'

Iona stood for a moment gazing out at the loch. 'I'd happily live here forever,' she said, sighing.

'You should try,' he said, admiring her as she looked at the countryside surrounding them.

'In another life,' she murmured, almost to herself.

If it was in his power to give her that life, he would surely try.

'Without wishing to pry,' he began, 'what type of life do you have to go back to? It's okay if you'd rather not tell me. I'm sure you have your reasons for taking this job. I assume something made you want to leave your home and come all the way up here.'

'I don't have anything to hide, not from you.' She felt he wouldn't make her feel awkward, or as if she'd never achieved anything special. 'I left little behind. My parents are long gone, and I'd been sharing a flat that never felt like home. I'd had various jobs, mostly in haberdashery as I've always loved sewing and quilting, but I never felt settled. As if I was always in the wrong place at the wrong time. I guess it was inevitable that I'd date Mr. Wrong types.'

Kier nodded, taking in every word, piecing together the patchwork past that had never been right for her.

'When I saw this job advertised, I jumped at the chance, and Jinette took me on without even meeting me. I applied online and we spoke on the phone, then I packed my bags and moved here to live and work in the shop.' She gazed out over the loch. 'It's so lovely here. I live in a large town that feels like a city, but I've always pictured myself at home in the wilds.'

He smiled. 'Well, maybe things will change for the better and you'll end up staying here.' He lifted the quilt from the car and spread it on the grass near the edge of the loch. 'But for now, let's have lunch. I hope you're hungry.'

'I am. I was up early again, so breakfast seems like ages ago.'

'An early riser like myself.' He started to set up their picnic style lunch.

The bakers had supplied them with napkins, and Iona helped him arrange their bridies and cupcakes on the napkins and set them on the quilt.

'I've been getting up with the larks since I arrived here. At home I tend to hide under the duvet even after the alarm goes off,' she confessed. 'I think it's living in the cottage, having a garden to step out into at breakfast and feeling as if I can breathe here. The pace is slower, and yet...'

'You've been a busy bee since you arrived?' he said smiling at her.

She nodded and smiled back at him. 'I certainly have. The sewing bee nights are buzzing with chatter and excitement.' Then she felt the blush rise in her cheeks. 'And look where I am now, with you. This afternoon I'll have some catching up to do with the shop orders.'

'Nope,' he cut–in. 'Jinette says you can happily abscond for the whole afternoon.'

She glanced at him. 'Did she?'

'Phone her if you don't believe me, but I made a bid for you to spend the afternoon with me. Hessie and Airlie are helping her.'

It felt like a weight had been lifted from her. She didn't feel guilty leaving Jinette to tend the shop on her own.

Kier poured two cups of tea and handed one to Iona. 'Let's propose a tea toast.'

Iona smiled and held up her cup. 'What shall we drink a toast to?'

Kier didn't hesitate. 'To you finding a way to never going home. To making this your home.'

'I'll certainly drink to that.' She tipped her cup against his, and noticed how his beautiful grey eyes looked at her. Friends with potential? Oh yes, perhaps she had a future here after all?

CHAPTER SEVEN

After their picnic lunch, Iona lay back on the quilt, gazed up at the bright blue sky and relaxed listening to the water on the loch lap gently against the edges. The long grass wafted in the breeze.

She sighed and smiled. 'This is lovely. Sooo relaxing. I don't think I've relaxed since I started work at the quilt shop. No complaints. I've been happily busy, but it's nice to unwind on a day like this.'

'A long, hot summer is predicted,' Kier said, lying down to join her.

Iona smiled.

'I'm not hinting at anything,' he told her.

And then his phone rang. He ignored it. 'They can leave a message.'

'Take the call,' she insisted. 'I don't mind. It could be important.'

He had a rough idea what it would be. 'Yes?' He listened while one of his workers explained the predicament. 'Okay. I'll deal with it. Thanks for calling.'

Iona sat up. 'Everything okay?'

'That was one of my workers. I've had an extra order for a delivery of flowers. We have them available, but I have to oversee the process.'

'That's fine. Drop me off at the shop. We've had lunch, and I had a nice time.'

Kier sat up and looked at her. 'Come with me.'

'To your fields?'

'To the farmhouse. I have to okay the paperwork and other things. It won't take long.' He picked up the empty flask. 'We can have another round of tea — and more cake.'

'Cake?' Iona smiled. 'How could I refuse?' she joked.

Kier stood up and held out his hand. She clasped her hand in his and felt his strong grip help her to her feet. She was now standing close, gazing up at him. Her senses reacted to his masculinity, and she stepped back and began to tidy up.

She shook the grass from the quilt, folded it and put it in the back of the car while he tidied up their picnic items.

Kier drove them the fairly short distance to his estate, taking the narrow road that led to his large, white farmhouse. Apple trees created a canopy of welcome shade in an area of the substantial garden. Trailing roses grew near the front door, and the window boxes on the ground floor were filled with flowers, especially pansies of all colours. Blue lobelia dominated the hanging baskets at the entrance, and he had a well–cut lawn that stretched round to the back garden.

'You have a beautiful house, Kier,' she remarked, admiring the two storey farmhouse that looked like it belonged on the front cover of a stylish lifestyle magazine. The white painted exterior and grey roof was set within a cultivated garden that was edged on all sides by his flower fields. The bright colours of the flowers looked picturesque in the bright sunlight, and she could see a handful of workers tending to the fields.

'I can drop you off at the house,' he offered. 'Or you can come with me while I deal with this order and then we can head to the house.'

'I'll go with you,' she said, eager to watch him at work, to understand his business, and to enjoy seeing the flowers.

'Great, it shouldn't take long.' He smiled over at her and drove the car round the rear of the farmhouse and onwards along the edge of a field where one of the workers, a mature man who seemed to be in charge of what was happening, came to meet him.

Kier pulled up, got out of the car and went over to talk to the man. Iona could hear snippets of their conversation and heard that a late order had come in from one of their regular clients. Apparently, the client supplied flowers for weddings, and one of their sources had let them down. Knowing that Kier was always reliable, they'd contacted him for the wedding flower order. A rush job, but Kier's workers were already gathering what was needed. They required Kier's approval before the flowers could be loaded up and driven by van to the supplier somewhere in the nearest large town.

She watched Kier flick through the paperwork, signing off on the documents, checking that everything was correct, and then smiling and thanking his workers for their efficiency.

Then Kier walked back to the car. Iona couldn't help admiring his long–legged stride and confident stature. He was a handsome man indeed. She could hardly believe that she was there with him. But she liked Kier, more than liked him.

He got into the car and reversed it up the narrow road, clearly used to navigating this.

Iona had a good view of the back garden. It was as well tended as the front garden, and there seemed to be a wooden structure, like a summerhouse, being built at the bottom of it.

'Are you building at summerhouse?' she asked him.

'Sort of. I haven't decided whether to keep it light and airy for the fine weather or make it a bit more durable so that it's cosy during the colder seasons,' he explained. 'The laird, Broden, has a winterhouse in the mansion's garden and I've always wanted to have something like that. I started work on it in the spring, but I've been so busy I haven't finished it yet. But I will.'

'A winterhouse? Oh, that sounds wonderful.' She pictured it would be cosy during cold days when it rained or snowed.

His face lit up hearing her enthusiasm. 'Do you think I should aim for a winterhouse?'

'An autumnhouse at the very least,' she said lightly.

He laughed. 'I've never heard of one of those, so...' he nodded firmly. 'An autumnhouse it is.'

'But capable of weathering the worst that a Scottish winter can throw at it.' She wouldn't want him wasting his plans due to her comments.

'Definitely. It'll withstand rainy days, frost and snowfall. I'll insulate it and make it snug as a bug.'

'While keeping it airy for summer days like this.'

He pretended to frown. 'You're a hard taskmaster, Iona. But, okay. It will be done to your satisfaction.'

Her heart squeezed when he smiled over at her, and pulled the car up at the back garden. For a moment, just a moment, she pictured herself with Kier, living at the farmhouse with him, and spending long afternoons in the autumnhouse sewing her quilts. Sheer bliss. Then she shook herself from her wayward thoughts and smiled back at him.

'We'll go in this way,' he said, getting out of the car. 'I'll show you the back garden.'

She got out and wandered around, admiring the flowers, and the path that cut through the lawn was edged by border plants in full bloom.

'Come and have a look at the autumnhouse,' he beckoned to her.

She hurried to catch up as he strode towards the half built structure.

They stood in the middle and he explained his plans. 'It'll look more like a cottage than a shed when it's complete.'

'Perfect.' She walked around picturing how homely it would be.

She caught him gazing at her, as if she was perfect in his eyes. She started to blush, and then wandered around the garden.

'Your roses are gorgeous,' she remarked, bending down, cupping one of the old–fashioned roses and breathing in the aroma.

'I love traditional flowers.'

She nodded and went over to admire the array of jasmine, hellebore and other flowers. 'What's that? It's a beautiful lilac colour.'

'Heliotrope.'

'Ah, it's very nice.' She thought about the floral embroidery kits in the shop. 'I think heliotrope is included in the quilt shop's embroidery patterns.'

'I suppose you're into embroidery.'

'Mainly quilting, and some dressmaking, but I'm adding to my embroidery skills. Jinette has shown me how to do quilt embroidery and I think I'm going to be hooked on that. And I'm embroidering floral patterns from the kits.'

'There's nothing better than working at something you truly love,' he said.

Iona agreed. 'I love my work. And obviously so do you.'

'We're both fortunate in that sense.' His words hung in the warm air, as if needing something added.

She gazed round at him and saw a flicker of melancholy in his eyes. It was there and gone in a moment. She sensed that he was sort of in the same position as her. Work was ideal, but love was elusive. Without both, life would always be less than either of them would want.

He shrugged off his deepest thoughts and invited her in. 'Let's get the kettle on, and then I'll give you a tour of the fields, if you'd like.'

She nodded excitedly. 'That would be great.'

They went in through the back door that led to the kitchen. She hadn't imagined she'd be there, in his house, but it was fascinating to see inside the property. His kitchen was impressive, decorated in pale grey and white, with all the modern equipment and gadgets, clean and tidy.

'I had my groceries delivered this morning so the cupboards are well stocked.' He opened the fridge door. 'Including a sponge cake with fresh cream and...' he peered in to see what the fruit filling was... 'raspberries.'

She laughed.

'I always order a cake and leave it up to them to select whatever they have. It's a local shop. They know my tastes.'

'It looks delicious,' she said.

'Right, let's get a cuppa organised—' His phone rang, interrupting him.

Iona nodded for him to take the call.

He sighed, slightly annoyed that he kept being thwarted. He checked the caller ID, sighed again, and then said to Iona, 'I have to take this one. It won't take long.' He eyed the kettle. A less than subtle hint.

She smiled. 'I'll put the kettle on to boil.'

He gave her the thumbs up as he accepted the call. He walked away through to the lounge. It didn't seem like a personal call, but she didn't want to eavesdrop, and ran the water extra forcefully to fill the kettle so she wouldn't be tempted to listen in.

However, as she flicked the kettle on, there was enough quietude to overhear him say...

'You have to stop calling, Margeaux. It's over. I'm not interested. I don't want to sound cold and blunt, but you won't seem to take no for an answer.'

Margeaux? An ex–girlfriend? Possibly. A pang of jealousy stabbed through her. An unfamiliar feeling, and unwarranted.

He seemed to go quiet, as if listening to whatever Margeaux was saying without interrupting her.

Iona unhooked two mugs from a rack and set them down on the kitchen table, quietly, as the urge to eavesdrop got the better of her.

'Okay,' he relented. 'One night next week. Yes, I'll arrange dinner reservations at the usual hotel. But I warn you, I won't change my mind. And I won't be staying overnight.' He ended the call abruptly and she heard him come back through.

The mugs rattled on the kitchen table as Iona's hand knocked against them in her rush to grab two small plates for their cake. She lifted the plates from a shelf and pretended she hadn't heard anything.

'The kettle's almost boiled,' she said, forcing herself to sound chirpy, while her heart felt totally crushed. The excitement and anticipation of seeing Kier's fields, having a look around his house, and spending the afternoon with him had gone. Now all she wanted to do was find an excuse to cut short her visit and head back to the quilt shop. To the safety of her sewing, the shop, cheery chatter with Jinette and the customers. And forget that she'd foolishly let her thoughts run away with her. How ridiculous she must seem. A rich, handsome and successful man like Kier was sure to have women throwing themselves at him. She felt like she was no more than a new bit of interest for him. The new girl in the village. His heartbreaker reputation was now making sense. And she'd let herself fall for it. Shame on her. Shame on him if that was all he was after. Yet, he'd seemed so genuine. Perhaps that was the problem. He was telling the truth. He was interested in her, he liked her, but as for having a happy future, something that would last, she assumed she could forget it. Kier was a handsome distraction. No wonder he lived on his own.

The kettle clicked off the boil. They both reached for it, and as their hands touched, she immediately pulled her hand away from his.

He didn't miss her reaction. A look crossed his face. He realised she'd overheard the conversation. The atmosphere in the kitchen had changed, the happy playfulness between them had gone, replaced with her wariness.

He sighed heavily. 'Margeaux is a client.'

Iona fussed with the tea, grabbing a teapot and pouring water over the teabags, barely glancing at him. She hated feeling jealous, but she loathed being taken for a fool. Though it was her own fault. She never picked nice men. She always made bad choices when it came to men. So here she was yet again, standing in a fairytale that was destined not to have a happy ending.

'It's none of my business.' She stirred the tea and put the lid on the pot to let it brew.

'I'd like to make it your business. If we're to have any chance at...'

She looked up at him. 'At what?' She shrugged as if it was inevitable that he'd try to sweet talk her into believing him.

'At perhaps taking things further than friendship. Taking it slowly, as I understand you've been hurt in the past.'

She didn't have the strength to react. Her stomach was knotted and she felt slightly teary. And angry with herself, while trying to hide all of it from him.

He ran a frustrated hand through his thick blond hair. 'I know how this looks, how this sounds. But you can trust me, Iona. I'm not involved with Margeaux. I never have been, even though she's tried to change my mind. And I never will be.'

'Dinner reservations at the usual hotel?' Her words were clipped and intentionally curt.

He didn't miss her meaning. 'You're right. That does sound like a rendezvous. But it's not.'

'I think I'd like to go back to the shop.' Her tone left no room for persuasion to stay.

He nodded, his heart heavy. 'I'll drive you.'

'I'd prefer to walk. It's not far.' She walked out of the kitchen into the back garden and headed round to the front of the house. She could see the narrow road they'd driven down. If she headed along there it would lead her straight back to the village. The walk would do her good, far more good than staying and pretending everything was fine with Kier. If there was one thing she'd learned from the broken relationships in her past, it was better to leave than linger.

Kier hurried through to the front door. He stood there, pressing his fist to his lips to prevent himself from calling after her. He watched her walk away. Beautiful Iona. It tore his heart apart to watch her slight figure disappear along the road.

He kicked himself for causing her to be upset, but he didn't blame her. He should never have agreed to meet with Margeaux, even if it was for business, and to make clear to her for the last time that he was never going to become romantically involved with her.

'Everything okay, Kier?' the older worker asked him, walking over and seeing Iona walk away.

Kier shook his head, and swallowed his upset. No, it wasn't okay. He feared it never would be between him and Iona ever again.

'I know it's none of my business, Kier,' the man began, 'but Iona seems like a lovely young lady. If I were you, I'd fight to make things right with her.'

Kier glanced at the man. They'd known each other for a long time, since Kier was a young boy.

The man didn't saying anything else. He simply nodded encouragement to Kier, as if to say — go on, hurry after her, don't let her slip through your fingers. This young woman is worth fighting for. So fight for her!

A wave of determination washed over Kier. He nodded and then ran after her. His car was still parked out back, but he didn't think to get it and drive because the urge to run was overwhelming.

'Iona!' Kier shouted, but his words were blown away by the sudden breeze that had picked up. The weather in the afternoons could change so fast, and the brisk wind coming in over the hills swept down across the fields of his estate, blowing the flowers in the breeze.

Iona fished out her phone from her bag. She felt the need to phone Jinette, to tell her what had happened. She was so cut, hurt and overwhelmed and—

'Iona! Wait,' Kier shouted.

She heard his voice in the distance. Her heart reacted. Part of her wished he'd let her walk way, and part of her hoped he'd try to coax her back.

She decided to keep walking, looking along the road, seeing nothing but beautiful countryside that in other circumstances would've been wonderful to stroll past. But here she was, close to tears, trying to concentrate on her phone to call Jinette.

'I'm sorry, Iona!' Kier's voice rang clear in the warm breeze.

She swept her hair back from her face and realised she had tears rolling down her cheeks. She barely realised. Wiping them away, she hurried on.

The sound of a vehicle made her look round. She caught a glimpse of Kier running down the road, and a bakery van driving past him to get to her.

The van slowed and the driver called out the window. 'Want a lift, Iona?'

Her heart cheered when she saw it was Gairn.

She didn't hesitate. 'Yes,' she said, climbing in the passenger side. 'Take me back to the shop please.'

Without a backwards glance at Kier, she nodded to Gairn.

He sussed out the situation and drove off before Kier could catch up.

Iona glimpsed the figure of Kier standing far behind them. Just standing there, watching her drive off with Gairn. Her heart ached.

Gairn didn't ask if everything was okay. Clearly it wasn't. 'Do you want to talk about it?' he offered.

Normally, she kept her feelings buttoned up, but Gairn made her feel like she could confide in him. So she did. She told him everything that had happened.

'Are you sure you don't want me to take you back to talk to him?' Gairn offered.

Iona shook her head. 'I think I need to go home. To the shop,' she added quickly, forgetting that her real home was far way.

Gairn picked up on her remark. 'It's your home, for now, for the summertime.' He smiled gently. 'I'll take you home. Everything will be fine with a bit of time. Things will work out the way they were meant to be.'

She smiled gently at Gairn. And then gazed out the window as the countryside filtered past. Fields of flowers in the distance swayed gently in the breeze. Oh how she'd longed to tour Kier's fields and not have her hopes shattered yet again.

Gairn drove them the fairly short distance back to the main street. Iona sat quietly. She looked pale, and yet she seemed to have caught a touch of the sun on her face. He'd been out delivering cakes and bakery goods to customers and was heading back to the village.

He dropped her off outside the quilt shop.

'Thank you, Gairn,' she said, giving him a look that thanked him for more than the lift. For his kindness and tact too.

Jinette was surprised to see Iona back so soon. 'You're back early.'

Iona nodded. She still looked pale, while Jinette's cheeks were flushed pink.

Hessie and Airlie were in the shop stitching quilts and having tea. It seemed as if they'd all been sitting having tea and chatting.

'You look...flustered,' Iona said to Jinette.

Hessie guffawed.

Airlie snickered and could hardly sew for trying to contain her laughter.

'Did something happen?' Iona asked them, forgetting her own woes for a moment.

'Oh, yes!' said Hessie.

'Nothing happened,' Jinette cut–in. Then she said to Iona, 'You just missed Lochty. He popped in to give me a wee minding to celebrate our engagement.'

Airlie burst out laughing. 'He was giving you a lot more than that, Jinette, by the sounds of it.'

'They were *kissing* in the kitchen when we arrived,' Hessie told Iona, winking.

Jinette looked like her cardigan was ruffled and straightened it brusquely. 'It was only a wee peck on the cheek.'

Hessie's eyes widened. 'A wee peck? Lochty sounded as if he was in full woodpecker mode.'

Iona smiled, and the women giggled. Even Jinette tried not to smirk and her cheeks became even brighter pink.

'Lochty was giving me a wee token of his affection,' Jinette explained. She held up a bag of chocolates. 'He bought these special chocolates from the bakers. Gairn made them. Lochty's planning to give me something else after dinner tonight.'

Airlie let go a loud snort. 'I bet he is!'

Jinette gave Airlie a scolding look, but couldn't contain her own laughter. 'We might have had a wee kiss and cuddle in the kitchen, but nothing happened.'

The cheery atmosphere lifted Iona's spirits and she found herself smiling again.

'So what happened with you and Kier?' Jinette asked.

Iona helped herself to a cup of tea and joined them in their chatter. She told them every detail of her date with Kier.

'Margeaux?' Jinette gasped.

'You know her?' Iona asked.

'Oh, yes, I know her.' Jinette shook her head in disapproval. 'She's a right vixen.'

'Isn't she the one that was after Kier?' Airlie said to Jinette.

Jinette nodded. 'She's the one that came into my shop to pick up information about Kier so she could worm her way into his affections.'

Hessie chimed–in. 'She was a real snooty nose type. Looked down her nose at us. She came in one night when we were having our sewing bee, and stared down at us as if quilting and sewing was beneath her.'

'She was cheeky,' Airlie recalled. 'Seemed very confident. A city type businesswoman. Jinette put her out.'

Iona blinked. 'You put her out of the shop?'

Jinette buttoned up her cardigan. 'I did. Cheeky madam. Kier's not interested in her. But she's got the hots for him and thinks she's got the looks to snare him.'

'And has she? Got the looks?' Iona asked.

Jinette typed at the keyboard of the shop's computer. She accessed a website, a business. Margeaux was head of marketing. 'There she is.'

Iona looked at the picture that accompanied Margeaux's bio on the website. 'She looks like a model.'

'She does,' Jinette remarked, and then flicked the link to the website off. 'We've better things to do than admire her smirking face.'

Iona had pictured that Margeaux would be a sleek, elegant, dark haired businesswoman, impeccably dressed. And that was what she saw on the website.

'Why isn't Kier interested in her?' Iona asked them. 'She's definitely got the looks, and has her own success.'

'She's not nice.' Jinette shrugged. 'It's as simple, or as complicated, as that.'

'Kier would never want to date a cold–hearted beauty,' Hessie said to Iona.

'So why would he agree to have dinner with her, at a hotel?' Iona asked them.

'Margeaux's company is one of Kier's main clients,' Jinette explained. 'She puts a lot of business, via the company she works for, his way.'

'But ultimately, Kier doesn't need their business,' said Airlie. 'From what I hear, Kier doesn't need any of them.'

Jinette agreed. 'It's convenient for him to do business with main clients rather than lots of little businesses. But he'll cut her company out as a client if she persists in harassing him. He told me that himself when he heard I'd shown her the door that night at the sewing bee.'

Hessie frowned at Iona. 'Did Kier not explain the situation to you?'

Iona sighed. 'I sort of didn't give him a chance. I...I ran off, and Gairn picked me up. Kier was running after me. Perhaps if I hadn't gone with Gairn—'

'Hush now!' Jinette said, curtailing Iona upsetting herself. 'Kier won't give up on you that easily. I know him. Trust me. If he likes you, he'll make amends for any misunderstanding.'

'Did he really agree to have dinner with Margeaux?' Hessie asked Iona.

Iona nodded. 'I heard him make the date with her, but he told her he wasn't interested in her, and had no plans to stay overnight at the hotel.'

Airlie looked suspicious. 'What was he thinking of booking a reservation at a hotel? He owes you a proper explanation.'

Jinette looked at Hessie and Airlie with a glimmer of doubt. 'He wouldn't be secretly dating Margeaux, would he?'

The women agreed that he wouldn't. But the feeling of doubt lingered in the shop.

'I'll make another round of tea for us,' Jinette said, trying to sound cheerful. 'The next time you speak to Kier, hear him out. Then decide if he's telling the truth or not.'

Iona nodded, but she was glad to be back at the quilt shop, in the company of the ladies, having tea and biscuits, and getting on with her quilting.

CHAPTER EIGHT

Iona cut floral print cotton fabric for a customer in the quilt shop. The shop was quite busy. The afternoon flew in, and she tried not to think about what had happened earlier with Kier.

'Are these the new fabrics for quilting?' another customer asked Iona while she was working at the cutting table.

'Yes,' Iona told her. 'You can buy them off the roll, or we have fat quarter bundles ready cut with a mix of floral cotton prints from the new fabric collections.'

The customer smiled. 'The bundles would suit me. I'm starting a new quilt, and I heard that the shop had new fabrics in.' She viewed the bundles. 'These are so pretty. Yes, I'll have one of these. Do you have backing fabric to go with it?'

Iona nodded. 'We have extra wide fabric in colours to tone in with the bundles that are ideal for quilt backings.' She finished cutting the floral fabric, folded it neatly, and then attended to the second customer's order.

Unrolling the wide backing fabric that was a small print in pastel tones, Iona saw Lochty heading towards the shop. 'Here's Lochty.'

Jinette was helping a customer select yarn to knit a cardigan, and smiled as he hurried in, looking eager to tell her something.

'That's our engagement party booked at the mansion,' Lochty announced. 'Tavish confirmed the booking with me. They're going to handle all the party food and preparations.'

Tavish worked for Broden, the laird, as one of his hotel reception staff and general worker. Lochty often did handyman jobs for Broden and they got on very well.

'Wonderful!' Jinette smiled and looked excited.

Lochty took a deep breath. 'Broden wants to give us the party, on the house, as an engagement present.'

Jinette's eyes widened. 'Broden's still away on business. Did someone tell him we're engaged?'

Lochty nodded. 'Tavish and a few others. We're the talk of the village.'

'Oh, that's very generous of Broden,' said Jinette. She glanced at Iona. 'I hope you get to meet the laird. He's a lovely man. Broden is very wealthy and looks after the community whenever he can. He takes his responsibilities as laird seriously. Broden and Kier both grew up here, so they're around the same age. Sometimes they have wee skirmishes, mainly silly jealousies, but we're fortunate to have such generous benefactors in our village.'

'So Kier contributes to the village too?' Iona asked.

'He does. Kier gave us the big Christmas tree we had last year and paid for all the lighting and decorations in the main street,' Jinette told Iona. She giggled. 'Broden is always Santa and dresses up to give out gifts locally, and we have a Christmas party at his mansion. Kier is relegated to dressing as a reindeer. Sometimes that causes a stooshie between them.' She laughed. 'The two of them were fighting in the snow when Eevie first arrived to work at the shop. She didn't know what to think of them. Then of course, she ended up dating the laird. She's friends with Kier, but there's no romance between them.'

Iona took in every word, picturing how wonderful the village would look at Christmastime covered in snow. And she thought about Kier. The more things she found out about him, the more she was in a quandary. Should she phone him and talk things over? Or should she leave things to calm down?

Airlie had gone home, but Hessie had stayed to help out at the quilt shop. She emerged from the rear of the shop laden with a large roll of quilt wadding from the cupboard.

Lochty grinned at Hessie. 'Tavish is planning to ask you to go with him to our engagement party.'

Hessie unrolled the wadding and proceeded to cut pieces for a customer's order. 'Is he now?' She smiled to herself.

'You should go with him, Hessie,' Jinette said, putting the customer's yarn in a bag along with a complimentary knitting pattern for a cardigan. The customer left happily with their yarn and free pattern.

Hessie continued the cutting and shrugged. 'I know we've been out a couple of times for a wee bite to eat, and we were dancing at one of the mansion's functions, but...I feel my days for romance are fading. I'm content with my quilting.'

'Nonsense,' said Jinette. 'Look at Lochty and me. You and Tavish could enjoy the same type of happiness as us. And Tavish is far better behaved than my Lochty.'

Lochty didn't argue with Jinette. He knew he could be a rascal from time to time.

Hessie straightened her shoulders. 'I'll think about it,' she relented.

Lochty clapped his hands together gleefully. 'Great. I'll tell Tavish he's got a date for our party.'

Hessie smiled and finished cutting the wadding.

Lochty then smiled at Iona. 'So that leaves you, Iona. But I'm sure Kier will be waltzing you round the dance floor at the celebration.'

Behind Iona's back Jinette was signalling to Lochty, trying to get him to stop assuming that Kier would take Iona to the party as his date.

Lochty frowned. 'Did I say something out of turn?'

Jinette sighed. 'I'll explain to you later. Now on you go. We're up to our eyeballs in orders. It's a very busy day.'

'Will I organise something for our dinner?' Lochty offered.

Jinette smiled and nodded. 'That would be handy.'

Lochty grinned. 'Anything special you fancy, apart from me?'

'Och, away you go.' Jinette giggled and shooed him out of the shop.

Lochty left with a spring in his step, and with plans to buy a pack of wedding invitations from the wee shop that sold everything on his way back to Jinette's cottage. Another surprise for her. They could sit and write out the invitations together and watch the telly.

More customers came in to buy fabric, embroidery kits and the latest locally dyed yarn. Iona, Jinette and Hessie were kept busy until closing time.

Iona bundled up some of the orders. 'I'll take these over to the post office and come back for the rest.'

Before she had finished gathering them, Jinette's phone rang. It was Milla from her dressmaker's shop that was part of the post office.

'Jinette, I know you're busy,' said Milla, 'but you have to come over to see what's just arrived at my shop.' The excitement in Milla's tone was obvious.

'What is it?' Jinette asked, eager to hear what it was.

'It's better to see than have me explain. Pop over. It'll only take five minutes,' Milla encouraged her.

'Okay, I'm on my way,' Jinette told Milla.

'What is it?' Hessie asked.

'I have no idea.' Jinette picked up the rest of the parcels. 'Come on, Iona, I'll go with you to the post office. Milla must have something really special to show me.'

Hurrying across, trying to guess what it might be, Iona and Jinette went into the post office part of the premises and handed the parcels over. They had an account with the post office, so all they had to do was put them down and leave the staff to handle it.

Jinette and Iona then went over to where Milla owned the clothes part of the post office. Milla's shop was partitioned off. The small shop was packed with dresses hanging on rails. Milla smiled when she saw Jinette and Iona.

'Look what arrived from my courier,' Milla announced and gestured to three large boxes filled with clothes.

Iona and Jinette went over to the table where the boxes were sitting and peered in.

'Vintage dresses!' Jinette exclaimed, having a rummage through one of the boxes.

Iona lifted one of the dresses from another box. It was a wrap dress with a floral rose print. 'This is a genuine vintage tea dress. 1940s or 1950s.'

Milla was beaming. 'I know. They were a job lot that no one wanted. One of my suppliers offered them to me for a real bargain. No one cared about their value. But look at them. Most of them are suitable for upscaling, or used for vintage quilting. I thought you'd be interested. I could bring some along to the next sewing bee night and we could all share them around.'

Iona lifted another of the dresses out and held it up in front of herself, viewing it in the full length mirror. The navy and white polka dot fabric draped beautifully and the skirt had box pleats that fell from the fitted waistline. 'This is gorgeous. Someone must've had these in storage and you've been lucky to get them.'

Milla nodded excitedly. 'They're from two sources, so there's a great mix of sizes. I've a feeling that one lot is from a shop's stock, and the other is a private buyer, maybe a fashionable woman had these hanging in her wardrobe. Some of them seem like they've only been worn a few times. But others are in need of repair.'

Jinette inspected one of the slightly damaged dresses. 'This could be repaired around the collar with embroidery.'

'That's what I thought,' Milla agreed. 'Any marks or holes could be repaired with a bit of embroidery or creative mending. I'll put them all through the wash tonight so they're fresh and clean.'

Milla often bought second hand dresses and upscaled them, so she knew how to carefully wash them, but she'd never had so many dresses in one order.

'You could resell these and make a nice wee profit,' Jinette said to Milla.

Milla shook her head. 'I've neither the time or the room in the shop to handle all of these.' She pointed to one of her dress racks. 'I'm fully stocked with summer dresses, skirts and tops. I'd have to take these home. And there's barely room for me in my own house these days because of all the dressmaking that's taken over.'

Iona knew that feeling. Her room at the flat contained her fabric stash, and it had slowly taken over her wardrobe. She hadn't brought any of her stash with her because Jinette said there was plenty of fabric in the shop that she could use for her quilting.

'Besides,' Milla continued. 'You're always sharing your fabric with us, Jinette. I'd like to share these with the sewing bee ladies. Let's all enjoy these vintage dresses. We could make so many things. I'd love to sew a vintage quilt with some of these fabrics.'

Iona studied one of the dresses. 'This dress is well–worn. Well–loved obviously, but it's past its best for wearing as a dress. But the fabric could be cut up for a beautiful and authentic vintage quilt.' Iona sounded as if she was picturing exactly what could be made from it.

Milla nodded.

'If you're sure,' said Jinette.

'I am,' Milla said firmly. 'I'll certainly upscale a couple of the dresses and sell them in my shop and online, but I'd rather share them out. It's too much work for me to tackle on my own.'

With this settled, Jinette and Iona hurried back to the quilt shop.

After explaining about the vintage dresses to Hessie, they closed the shop for the day.

Jinette quickly restocked one of the shelves with yarn from the cupboard. 'I'll alert the sewing bee ladies. We'll probably have an impromptu bee tomorrow night.'

Iona loved that the sewing bee night could be arranged to suit whatever was happening with the members.

'I'll finish tidying up,' Iona said to Jinette.

'Are you sure?' Jinette asked her.

'Yes, I'll see you bright and early in the morning.'

Iona waved to Jinette and Hessie as they left. She locked the door and made short work of restocking the shelves. Hessie had helped tidy the shop, so only a few things needed sorted before she could relax. And she really felt that she needed to unwind.

With everything tidied, she went through to the kitchen to make something for her dinner. Nothing fancy or fussy. There was a fresh, crusty loaf untouched, so she cut two thick slices and made a doorstep sandwich with cheddar cheese, lettuce, tomato and tomato pickle.

Pouring herself a mug of tea, she sat down at the kitchen table, opened the door wide to let the warm air from the garden in, and ate her dinner.

Early evening sunlight streamed in through the open door. The scent of the garden, along with the golden glow, soothed her senses. She bit into the sandwich and rewound the events of the day, especially the parts that included Kier.

Her heart ached when she thought about him. Maybe she wouldn't have reacted so impulsively if she hadn't been enjoying herself so much with him. Their time at the loch, lying on the heather beds, getting to know each other's pasts and presents. Then the excitement of visiting his farmhouse and the fields, those beautiful fields.

She sighed heavily and drank her tea to wash away the bitter taste of what happened when Margeaux phoned and spoiled everything.

Finishing her dinner, she wandered out into the garden to enjoy the last of the sunlight before it faded for the night. She couldn't help wondering what would've happened if Margeaux hadn't interrupted her visit to Kier's farmhouse. Would they have taken their relationship further than friendship? There was a strong attraction between them. She sensed it, especially when they'd stood in the half built autumnhouse. She would've loved to have stayed to enjoy tea and cake with him, see more of his lovely house, and tour the flower fields.

She was still mulling over everything when her phone rang. Few people in the village had her number, so it had to be someone from home, or Jinette or...

She checked the caller, and her heart jolted. It was Kier. Hesitating for a moment, she answered it.

'Iona, it's Kier,' he said tentatively, as if he was worried she'd hang up on him. 'Can I talk to you for moment?'

'Yes,' she said, softly.

She heard him sigh. 'I wanted to let you know that I'm leaving. I'll be back in a few days.'

'Okay.' She didn't know what else to say. He was leaving? Was he going to meet up with Margeaux?

'Gossip often exaggerates the truth, or slants it. I figured you'd hear that I'd left to go to the city, and you'd assume I was meeting up with Margeaux.'

'It's really none of my business what you do, or whoever you're with.'

He paused and chose his words carefully. 'I'd like to hope that when I come back, we could start again, without any misunderstandings or foolish moves on my part. That would make it your business, Iona. Because if we're to have any sort of future, I want to start things properly without baggage from my past causing us to quarrel.'

'I don't want to quarrel with you, Kier.'

'I'm glad. So I wanted you to hear it from me before all the gossipmongering. I'll be back in a few days. All I ask is that you trust me to do the right thing. Will you do that for me?'

'I will.' She paused, sensing the distance between them widening, knowing he was going away. 'Anything else you want me to do?'

'Yes. Try not to fall in love with Gairn or Aran while I'm away.'

She laughed lightly, nervously. 'Trust me to do the right thing.'

'I'll see you when I get home,' he murmured gently.

'Okay,' she said.

And then he was gone.

She put her phone away and gazed up at the darkening sky through the branches of the apple trees. Deep in thought about Kier's call, she was startled when she heard someone knock on the front door of the shop, and hurried inside.

She saw Aran standing outside the shop peering in. He smiled when she opened the door.

'I need your expert opinion on something.' He was carrying a quilt, neatly folded, and held it out to her. 'What colour of thread would look great with this? I'm about to machine quilt it, but the customer left a message saying they don't want the thread to blend in. I usually use a light grey because it blends in with everything — solids, prints, whatever the fabric or pattern. But they want something a bit different without being gaudy, so lime and burnt orange are out.'

'Hang on.' She hurried over to the thread display and lifted two spools of thread — a pale pink and a light aqua blue. 'I like to use these colours for my quilting. I still use grey sometimes, but I love the effect of these pastels.'

Aran held the pink next to the fabric. 'The pink could work.' Then he tried the blue. 'The blue is nice too.' He looked at Iona. 'What would you use? I really need to get this quilted tonight. The courier is picking it up first thing in the morning. And I've still to put the binding on.'

Iona studied the quilt — the fabric, the modern quilt blocks he'd so expertly pieced together, and made her decision. 'Blue. It'll enhance the summery feel of the fabric. It'll look great. I've used it so many times and it always works.'

Aran handed back the pink thread and kept the blue. 'I'll buy this. I've probably got something similar, but this will save me having to colour match it to thread from my range.' He fumbled to reach into his trouser pocket to pay her.

'It's fine,' she assured him, allowing him to hurry on.

'Thanks, Iona.' He rushed over towards his shop, but paused in the quiet road and called back to her. 'Are you going with anyone to Jinette and Lochty's engagement party?'

She sensed he'd heard about her falling out with Kier.

Aran seemed hopeful and handsome standing there looking at her.

'Maybe,' she called back to him.

Aran smiled at her answer, nodded and then hurried inside his shop.

Her non-committal reply had given him hope that maybe she would go with him as his date.

She closed the shop door and locked it again. And sighed heavily. Every time she paused to think about Kier, something interrupted her. It was as if she wasn't meant to become involved with him.

Shaking off her doubts, she went through to the kitchen to make more tea.

While the kettle boiled she gave in to temptation and looked at the website Jinette had shown her earlier. The one with the picture of Margeaux.

Studying the elegant beauty, so poised and confident, made her heart sink. She wished she hadn't looked again at the woman Kier was due to meet. He hadn't said he was meeting Margeaux. But she knew he was. She knew.

She heard the kettle boil, and flicked off the computer. Kier had asked her to trust him and she'd promised she would. But nothing felt settled. No wonder she'd put romance on the back burner.

After making a cup of tea, she sat in the shop and worked on her new quilt. Her favourite method was English paper piecing. Having selected the floral fabric bundle she wanted to use, she began to cut hexagon shaped pieces of fabric, using templates and pre–cut paper shapes. She'd always enjoyed making hexies. The process of thread basting the fabric around the paper shapes to create the small fabric hexies was relaxing. Once she had enough, her plan was to start hand stitching the edges of the hexies together in a lovely design to make the top layer of the quilt. The papers would be removed once the hexies were stitched together.

As the piles of hexies she'd made piled up on the table she was working at, that had a view of the main street, she tried not to think about Kier and Margeaux.

Thread basting the hexies, one by one, she kept glancing over at the sewing shop. The lights were on and she could see Aran sitting at his sewing machine, busy quilting.

Had he really needed her advice about thread colour, or was he using it as an excuse to talk to her? She shrugged off her doubts. Either way it didn't matter. She'd no intention of becoming involved with Aran.

Milla had mentioned that his shop hadn't attracted many local customers. Loyalty to Jinette's shop had been strong in the community. She supposed that given time, people would start to frequent his shop and buy from him as well as Jinette. He'd insisted that his online sales were high, so it really didn't matter where he was located. His online sales probably hadn't been affected at all, especially if he had a rush order for that quilt, and presumably other quilts and fabric sales.

The bakery shop was lit up too, though she couldn't see Gairn. He'd mentioned about working late at night, so he was probably busy in the kitchen. She pictured the delicious sweets he'd be making — everything from white chocolate truffles to dark chocolate fudge and caramelised cherries. His chocolate cake was the best she'd tasted in a long time. The village had lost its little sweet shop to the sewing shop, but it was sure to gain a master chocolatier when Gairn settled down to work at the bakery.

She was so deep in thought about the bakery that at first she didn't notice Aran waving over to her from his window. Then the frantic waving caught her attention. She put her sewing aside and peered out at him. Yes, he was insisting she come over.

So she did. She hurried over to Aran's shop.

'I'm sorry to disturb your sewing,' he said, sounding almost breathless. 'But could you have a look at the quilting I've done. I think it looks great with the blue thread, but I'd appreciate your input.'

Iona let herself be ushered quickly inside the sewing shop. It was bright and cheerful, and the scent of the original sweet shop gave it a homely feeling. It also made her want to eat chocolates, and she noticed that he'd refilled the cake stand with Gairn's wrapped chocolates to tempt customers and sweeten them up. With few customers, the chocolates were hardly touched. The gold foil wrapping glinted under the counter's spotlights.

'I'll ply you with chocolates once you give the quilt a look over,' he promised. Under the shop's spotlights his hazel eyes twinkled with a sexy mischief that affected her even though she tried to resist. His handsomeness was in stark contrast to Kier's cool blond looks and pale grey eyes. Aran reminded her of the rich tones of autumn with strands of burnished auburn highlighted in his brown hair. He looked like he'd been walking in the sunshine and had caught a light bronze tan, though she couldn't imagine when he'd done this because he was forever working away in his shop. All his hard work seemed to keep him in great shape, and the sinewy muscles in his forearms were evident as his shirt sleeves were rolled up.

She blushed, both from being caught eyeing the sweets, and from the way he stood so close to her, with a friendly familiarity — as if he'd known her for a long time, and was comfortable being around her.

Iona studied the stitching and was genuinely impressed. 'This is perfect.' The quilt had a modern design, quite arty she thought, with aqua, white, sea green and pastel tones in dramatic shapes.

He stood with his hands on his hips and sighed, like he'd been holding his breath, hoping she'd approve. 'I think I've nailed it. It's for one of my top clients, and they're going to put it up on their wall as a piece of art in the foyer of their advertising company.'

He held the quilt up and virtually disappeared behind it. All she could see were his toes and finger tips. 'Check that I haven't messed anything up. It'll mean I can sleep easy knowing it's finished to the standard they expect.'

'You can definitely sleep easy, Aran,' she said.

The look he gave her...admiring everything about her.

She started to blush and moved over to the chocolates. 'Did you have many customers today?'

'Nope. But it doesn't matter because my online sales rocketed.' He smiled and gestured towards the selection of chocolates. 'Help yourself to one of Gairn's specialities. I've indulged in a few myself, seeing as my customers are mainly in the city.' He lifted up a chocolate bonbon and popped it in his mouth.

'Do you think you'll miss the city?' she asked, and then ate a chocolate fudge sweet.

He nodded and finished eating his sweet. 'Yes, I'm missing it already, but it'll take time to find the right house here. Living in the shop premises, even though it's quaint and has all I need...' he shrugged. 'It doesn't feel like home. I need a house. I have my property agent, the one that dealt with me moving here, keeping a lookout for one in this area. Few cottages or houses are for sale in a small village like this, but when one is for sale, I'll buy it.'

He sounded so confident, assured that he'd find what he needed. There were people like that. Extremely self assured. She wasn't one of them.

'You're frowning,' he said.

'I was just thinking you're lucky to be able to settle down here.'

'So could you, if you really wanted to.'

It was her turn to shrug. 'Easier said than done.'

'Not if you met someone here — a man to settle down with.'

His suggestion hung in the air between them, and she felt quite overwhelmed. On one hand this would solve everything, but she prized her independence, making her own way in the world. At least she had until now. Was her stubbornness working against her? She did want to settle down.

'You're frowning again,' Aran said, smiling at her. 'Have another chocolate and stop thinking deep, dark thoughts.'

She unwrapped another chocolate sweet and bit into the rich chocolate truffle.

He smiled again at her, and she smiled back.

He nodded. 'That's better. You're too pretty to be wearing a frown.'

She couldn't hide her blushes.

Sensing that he may have overstepped the mark slightly, he invited her to try quilting a small mini quilt he'd been working on using his sewing machine.

'I know you like hand quilting, but try stitching this mini.' He ushered her over to his sewing table where his machine was set up.

'I'm concerned I'll mess it up for you.' She hesitated even though the urge to give it a go was strong. She was familiar with Jinette's machine in the shop. This was the latest model, but it wasn't too difficult to figure out how to navigate it, especially as Aran was right there leaning over her shoulder, offering encouragement.

'Go for it, Iona. Let rip.'

She laughed and did just that, surprising herself how adept she could be when she was concentrating like mad not to ruin it.

'Hey, you're either a secret machine quilter or you're just good at sewing,' he said, lifting up the mini quilt and admiring her handiwork.

'Neither. That was a fluke.' She stood up even though he wanted her to have another go. 'I'll quit while I'm ahead.'

'I admire your patience in hand quilting,' he said. 'I prefer the speed that a machine offers. I can stitch up a quilt in jig time in comparison to stitching it by hand.'

'I enjoy the slower pace. I like to relax while I'm quilting,' she explained. 'There are times when obviously I have to put a spurt on, and for something needed in a hurry I'll use a machine. But it's the gentle pace that appeals to me, and gives me time to think while I quilt.'

'I have to keep up with my customer's orders.'

She nodded. 'It's different if you own your own business.'

'Have you considered this for yourself?' he asked. 'Or thought of joining someone in business?'

'Jinette isn't looking for a partner in her quilt shop,' Iona told him.

He shook his head. 'I wasn't meaning Jinette.'

She realised he meant joining him at the sewing shop. The blush that had faded went into full flush again. Wow! This man could come on strong.

He held his hands up. 'Sorry, sorry again. I seem to be constantly apologising to you. It's just that...I'm going to be totally honest with you. I like you, Iona. I've liked you since I first saw you watching me from the window of the quilt shop.'

'I wasn't deliberately watching you,' she lied in her defence.

He tilted his head and gave her a knowing look. He knew she was lying.

'Okay, so I was intrigued because you kept yourself shuttered up when this village has a reputation for everyone knowing everyone else's business.'

'At least we're being truthful. So, with that said, I heard about the fiasco, sorry if that's blunt, with you and Kier. Your lunch date apparently didn't end well. It seems like Kier's reputation for being a heartbreaker is merited.'

'He phoned me. He's leaving for a few days, but he wants us to try again when he gets back.'

Aran took this news on the chin. 'All right, but I was hoping you'd like to go with me to Jinette and Lochty's engagement party. What do you say? Go with me. No strings. Just friends.'

'I sort of promised Kier I wouldn't...' Wouldn't what? Fall in love with Aran or Gairn while Kier was away? She couldn't tell Aran that even though they were both being straightforward.

Aran nodded, encouraging her to continue.

'I've decided to go to the party on my own. But that doesn't mean I won't dance with you at the party.'

'That's fair. I'll go along with that. But if you change your mind and want to go as my date, you know where to find me.'

'Almost surgically attached to your sewing machine,' she said lightly, trying to lift the conversation and stem her blushes.

He leaned close and smiled. 'I'm determined to turn you into a speedy machine quilter yet.'

'I'm determined to quilt by hand.'

He stood tall and extended his hand in a playful gesture. 'May the best quilter win.'

Iona shook his hand. 'I hope you're not a poor loser.'

He laughed. 'You don't give in easily, do you?'

'Never,' she replied, looking up at him and smiling.

A knock on the sewing shop window interrupted them. It was Gairn.

CHAPTER NINE

Kier drove through the night, wishing he'd done things differently. If Margeaux hadn't phoned... He shook his head.

Glancing at the passenger seat, he noticed he'd forgotten to bring his laptop. He muttered, angry with himself, and turned the car around to head back home to pick it up. He needed the laptop, and he hadn't driven too far from home to make it worthwhile popping back for it.

As he drove along the village's main street he noticed the lights were on in the quilt shop. His heart ached at the thought of Iona working away there, probably still upset with him.

He also noticed that the sewing shop and the bakery were lit up, though he didn't see any hint of Aran or Gairn.

Kier drove on, dwelling on thoughts of what might have been with Iona.

Parking outside his farmhouse, he ran in, picked up the laptop, and hurried back out.

He drove back along the main street. This time he saw Aran and Gairn standing outside the bakery, lit up from the glow of the shop windows. The lights shone out across the pavement — and his heart felt like it had been stabbed when he saw Iona standing there with them. Smiling, laughing.

He slowed down, but the three of them were so steeped in their cheerful conversation that they didn't notice his car drive past them.

Aran had rested his hand on Iona's shoulder. A light gesture perhaps, but a clear indication of his desire to possess her, to date her, and that she was comfortable with him. She didn't pull away, not that Kier saw.

But if he'd lingered for a moment longer, he'd have seen her step back and extricate herself from Aran while still maintaining the friendly chatter.

Kier glanced in the mirror and watched them as he drove away into the shadows. So much for her promise, he thought. Though perhaps she was just being friendly, nothing more. But no matter how hard he tried to convince himself that she'd wait for him, he couldn't help feeling like his heart had been ripped out and thrown aside in favour of Aran or Gairn.

Kier gripped the steering wheel and mentally kicked himself for everything he'd done wrong with Iona, beautiful Iona, then he concentrated on the road ahead as he drove off into the night heading for the city.

The cheery conversation between Iona, Aran and Gairn was concluding. Gairn had asked them to pop in to the bakery to sample his new chocolates, and then they'd headed back out and stood outside the shops.

'Those new chocolates were delicious,' Iona enthused to Gairn.

'Thanks for being the first testers,' said Gairn. 'When I heard the two of you laughing in the sewing shop, I thought I'd ask for your opinions.'

Aran grinned. 'Anytime, but I have to get back to my quilting.' He indicated towards his shop. 'I've still the binding to sew on.'

Gairn smiled and gestured. 'Yes, I don't want to keep you any longer from your work, Aran. I've chocolate layer cakes to bake.' He sounded as busy as Aran.

'I've never managed to bake a layer cake without it all squishing together,' said Iona. 'Maybe sometime you can give me a few tips.'

Gairn spread his arms wide. 'How about right now? Unless you have to rush back to the quilt shop?'

'No, I don't have to rush,' she told him. 'I was only stitching my quilt and relaxing.'

Gairn brightened. 'Great. Come back in and I'll show you an easy way to ensure your layers are perfect.' Then he smiled at Aran. 'Good luck with finishing your quilt.'

Aran smiled tightly. 'Thanks, Gairn.' He glanced at Iona and wished he hadn't mentioned that he needed to finish the quilt. He'd assumed she'd head back to the quilt shop. But no, now Gairn had snared her into the bakery, into a world of delicious chocolate and cakes.

Sweeping Iona into the bakery, Gairn smiled again at Aran, leaving him standing outside the sewing shop.

With slumped shoulders, Aran trudged inside and sat down at his sewing machine, in no mood to quilt anything.

Forcing himself to check he had enough thread on his bobbin to finish the quilting, he started to sew. The gentle purr of the machine sounded louder in the quiet shop, or perhaps it was the resonance of his inner ire.

Gairn led Iona through to the back of the bakery to where he'd been busy making the chocolates. He hadn't invited Iona and Aran into the kitchen, and had only given them a tasting of the chocolates at the front counter.

Iona gazed around. The kitchen was immaculate, and so well organised. The delicious scent of vanilla and chocolate filled the air.

Her hair was tied back in a ponytail, so it was out of the way for baking. His dark hair was well–cut, and she thought he suited the chef whites he was wearing.

'Here you go. Put this on.' He handed her a clean apron, sounding chirpy.

She put the white apron on and tied it around her waist. 'How do I look?' She was joking, thinking he'd say she was the ideal little helper, but instead he said something else entirely.

'You look beautiful, as ever.' The softness in his tone touched her heart.

She hesitated, taken aback, especially as his stunning blue eyes gazed at her. It was probably only for a second or two, but the connection felt longer, and the blush rose in her cheeks. She couldn't remember a time when she'd blushed so much, maybe not since she'd been a teenager venturing out with her friends on to the dating scene.

Gairn blinked out of the moment and fussed with the three round cake tins that he'd prepared. 'Right, first things first. We'll both have to scrub up.'

They went over to the double sinks and washed their hands, then went back to tackle the ingredients. The aroma of the chocolate was wonderful.

'Help me measure out the ingredients.' He made room for her to stand next to him as they worked side by side. She barely came up to his shoulders, but there was nothing about Gairn that made her feel small or insignificant. If she'd had to choose a male friend in the village, Gairn would be the top of her list.

'Do you create your own cake recipes?' she asked him as she sifted the cocoa powder and flour into a bowl.

'I do, and I plan to introduce more of my recipes when I've finished my training. However, this recipe is one of our traditional favourites based on my grandmother's baking. She taught my father how to bake.'

'It really is a family business then?'

'It is, but my father is keen to expand our product range — and that's where I come in. Or I will do once I come back for good.'

'Will you set up a sweet counter in the front shop?' she asked as Gairn got ready to add the butter, eggs, sugar and milk to the mixture.

'That was the original plan, but then we hoped to expand into the empty sweet shop. Now we're thinking of building an extension to the bakery out the back. The garden is quite long.'

They chatted while they worked. He revealed more about his plans, and he showed her how to mix the chocolate cake ingredients to create a smooth cake batter.

Iona enjoyed mixing the ingredients all together.

'Are you a hobby baker?' he asked her.

'Yes, and I'm fine with that, but I've always wanted to improve my basic sponge cakes, including chocolate cakes. So it's great to watch an expert at work.'

Gairn smiled, then scooped the cake mix into the three cake tins and popped them in the preheated oven. 'We'll leave these to cook for around thirty minutes while we make the chocolate buttercream.'

She learned that he used melted rich dark chocolate, butter, sugar, milk and cocoa powder to create the easy made but delicious buttercream filling for the cake.

'I'll often add other ingredients, a pinch of chilli powder, a splash of whisky or other flavourings.'

'The cake smells so tasty, and I know from having enjoyed the cake you gave us that your chocolate cakes are delicious.'

He smiled. 'We'll add chocolate dipped cherries to decorate it. You can pipe the buttercream on the top of the cake.'

'Me? You're trusting me with the piping?'

Gairn nodded. 'I certainly am.'

As the cakes were taken out of the oven and left to cool on a rack before the buttercream was added, Iona and Gairn sat together having a cup of hot chocolate. He'd grated a high quality chocolate on top of the frothy whipped cream.

'It's a nice night. Let's get some fresh air in the garden.' He led the way out of the kitchen into the back garden. The air was immediately refreshing.

She breathed in the calm night and gazed up at the stars in the dark sky. 'The stars shine so clear here, unlike the town where I'm from.'

'Or the city,' he added. 'Another benefit of living so far north, away from the city or large towns.'

She nodded and continued to gaze up at the stars, and again she felt that sense of being on the clock, that her time in the village was coming to an end, and this was something else she'd miss. The starry nights.

Her attention was pulled away from these thoughts as Gairn indicated where they planned to build the extension. 'We'll build outwards, from the rear of the bakery to over there near the flowers, and still have room in the garden for growing vegetables and herbs, or creating an outdoor area with tables and chairs for customers.'

His plans seemed firm. 'You've obviously planned well, but it's a pity you didn't get the sweetie shop. It would've been so handy for your business.'

The ambient evening light highlighted Gairn's classically handsome features and his eyes were like pale sapphires. And yet, her heart didn't yearn for him, for more than friendship.

'It would've been handy, but I think it's going to work out better for our business this way. It's made us rethink what we could reasonably do. Taking on the expense of buying a second shop would've affected our profits for a few years. We'd have made it up in the long run I suppose, but this way is within our budget.' He pointed up towards the roof. 'We're considering using the loft to transform it into a tea shop where I can have my chocolates and other sweet specialities.'

'That sounds great. A tea shop or tearoom would be lovely.'

'I wish I could open it now, but the summertime will fly in, and the autumn is an ideal time for launching a tea shop. I'll make little marzipan acorns dipped in chocolate, chestnut truffles, and decorate the cakes with milk chocolate leaves.'

'Will the tea shop be ready for the autumn?'

'Yes, my father and I will tackle flooring the loft and the reconstruction work needed soon. A couple of the local men, builders and joiners, will help us.'

'So you're a handyman as well as a baker and chocolatier?'

Gairn shrugged. 'My father taught me since I was a boy. They're useful skills to have, woodwork, putting up shelves, painting and decorating. I've always enjoyed working with my hands.'

A cool breeze blew across the garden, and she brushed the stray strands of hair back from her face. She didn't notice Gairn admiring her.

'I heard about you and Kier,' he said. It had been bugging him all night, wanting to tell her he'd heard about their argument.

She continued to gaze out at the garden. 'I suppose everyone's heard.'

'Gossip. Small village. Newcomer. Kier's reputation.' His bullet points summed it up perfectly.

Iona nodded. 'Kier's away for a few days. Maybe someone else will have become the hot topic by the time he gets back.'

'Like Aran, and you?' His blue eyes glinted as he looked at her.

'There's nothing going on between Aran and me.'

'Perhaps not from your side, but there's definitely plenty going on from him.'

She glanced at him.

'It's obvious that he's interested in you, Iona.'

'I'm not interested in Aran, not in that way,' she told him.

Gairn looked far into the distance. 'Aran won't settle here.'

Iona frowned. 'What makes you say that? Has he said anything about leaving?'

'No, but I've met men like Aran before, and they never settle down in quiet little villages like this. They may try, for a while, but eventually, they go back to the cities. They need the excitement, or what they perceive as excitement. Shopping malls, theatres, cinemas, restaurants, all the buzz.'

Gairn sounded so astute and insightful that she was intrigued and inclined to believe him. 'If Aran leaves, will you try to buy the sewing shop?'

'No. Our alternative plans are better, especially as I've said, regarding finances. We'd do better to expand our own property rather than get into debt with a second shop.'

'Aran could stay. You could be reading him all wrong.'

'I could, but I don't think so. We'll see.' He looked at her. 'Don't tell him I said this. I don't want to put ideas into his head or cause him to stay through sheer stubbornness and wanting to prove me wrong.'

'I won't say anything,' she promised.

Gairn drank down his hot chocolate. 'The cakes should be cool by now. Ready to tackle icing them with the buttercream?'

'No.'

He laughed. 'Come on. I'll show you how to pipe it on.'

Iona drank her hot chocolate too, then followed him inside. 'I don't even pipe buttercream on to my cupcakes because it skooshes everywhere except where I want it.'

'So what method do you use?'

'I sort of swirl it on and hide the wobbles with extra sprinkles,' she confessed.

He sucked the air in and pretended to disapprove as he smoothed the buttercream on to the cakes and layered them together. Then he scooped the buttercream into a piping bag and handed it to her. 'Do your worst. If it all goes wrong, we'll use your method of disguising it with sprinkles.'

He jokingly reached up to a shelf and brought down two large tubs of sprinkles.

Iona laughed.

'I'll keep these on standby.'

'Stop making me laugh,' she scolded him as she squeezed the first of the buttercream from the piping bag on to the top of the cake.

'That's it,' he said, encouraging her.

She used all the buttercream that was in the piping bag. 'I'm trying not to squidge it over the edge of the cake.'

'Using technical phrases like that will not earn you extra points,' he warned her jokingly.

'Ha! Now I'm determined to finish these last splodges...there, all done.' She put the piping bag down and feigned triumph. 'Marks out of ten?'

'Nine.'

She frowned at him.

'And a half.'

'I'll accept that.'

Gairn lifted the cake and put it in a white cake box. 'Accept this too.'

'I can't take your nice cake,' she said.

Gairn insisted. 'Take it for the sewing bee tomorrow night. I hear there's an extra meeting because of the vintage dresses that Milla has netted.'

'There really are no secrets around here.'

'None.' He handed her the cake box.

'I'll leave you to get on with your real baking work.'

'You're always welcome to pop over and join me. I'll have you whipping up chocolate ganache in no time.'

'I'll stick to quilting. It's not as delicious, but it's less messy.' She smiled and left him to get on with his baking.

The lights were still on in Aran's shop. She glanced in on her way to the quilt shop. She saw him busy cutting fabric, and decided to scurry past and head to the quilt shop.

'Iona!' Aran called to her.

She glanced back at him.

'How did the baking lesson go?'

Maybe she was overtired, but she picked up on a hint of jealousy in his tone.

She held up the cake box. 'My efforts are going to be eaten at the sewing bee tomorrow night.'

'I'm impressed,' he said.

She smiled and hoped he wouldn't invite her in to see whatever else he'd done with his quilting. She really was tired.

'I can see you're weary, so I won't keep you. I hope you enjoy whatever it is you'll do with Milla's vintage dresses.'

'We're planning to mend as many as we can. Others will be cut up and used for quilting,' she told him.

'Good luck with that. I'm not into make do and mend. I like the dresses I make, and my quilts, to be new, even if the styles are old–fashioned like my tea dresses. But I appreciate the quality of vintage clothes.'

'I love vintage. Pre–loved clothes have always interested me. And I enjoy make do and mend.'

He smiled, but it was obvious that the pre–owned vintage dresses were of no interest to him.

'Watching you sitting at my sewing machine quilting tonight made me realise that I need better lighting for sewing in the evenings. So, I've ordered new lights for the shop.'

Ordering new lights? This didn't sound like someone who was planning to leave. Maybe Gairn was wrong about Aran.

'Proper lighting is important, especially if you're sewing at night,' she agreed, and then made a move to leave.

'I'd better let you go. Thanks again for your help.'

'You're welcome, Aran.' She started to walk away.

The tiredness of the day was sinking in. She planned to put the cake in the kitchen and collapse into bed.

When she got back to the quilt shop, that's exactly what she did. Her hexies were still sitting on the table where she'd left them earlier. She figured she'd be up early and would tidy them away in the morning, or get more of them stitched.

Before flicking the computer off, she quickly checked the online orders. It seemed that they'd had a flurry of orders for the new embroidery kits, so she knew what she'd be busy packing up the next morning. The floral embroidery designs made her think about using some of them to mend the vintage dresses. The cherry blossom pattern would look perfect with the vintage dresses, so would several other floral designs including the pansy flowers, daisies and bluebells.

Lying in bed she felt herself drifting off easily as the tiredness kicked in. She thought about everything that had happened, and hadn't happened. Again, she pictured an alternative scenario if things had gone differently with Kier. Despite spending time with Aran and Gairn, it was Kier that occupied her thoughts as she fell asleep.

Kier couldn't sleep. The restlessness he felt was unfamiliar. He stood in his hotel room in the semi–darkness, lit only by the ambient glow of the moonlight shining in through the window. He'd gone to bed, but got up due to the restless feelings, and gazed out at the view of the city. The lights shimmered in the depths of the night. He couldn't ever remember feeling so unsettled.

His expensive grey silk pyjama bottoms hung low around his lean torso. He wore nothing else except a frown that deepened the grey of his eyes. The taut muscles showed across his broad shoulders. Shoulders that seemed to be carrying the extra weight of him missing Iona and not knowing what to do about it. He'd told her he'd do the right thing. He promised himself that he would try.

He hadn't known Iona long, but from the first time he'd seen her, he'd hardly stopped thinking about her, longing for her, eager to know her better and for her to know him. The real him, not the inaccurate image of him being a heartbreaker. If anyone's heart was in jeopardy it was surely his.

He thought again about Iona standing with Aran and Gairn, smiling, happy, relaxed in their company. Maybe he should've stopped his car instead of driving on. Another mistake he'd made.

He sighed wearily and continued to stand at the window gazing out at the glimmering lights, and wishing he could be with Iona.

CHAPTER TEN

Iona and Jinette were busy working in the quilt shop the next morning, packing up the orders.

Iona popped a lily of the valley embroidery kit into a bag as she told Jinette about Aran wanting her help to select thread for his quilt.

'I think we can afford to give Aran a spool of blue thread,' said Jinette as she folded the fabric orders. 'But tell me what happened when you went over to his shop.'

Iona explained everything, including Aran making a play for her.

'He's certainly very bold asking you to go to my party when he knows you're involved with Kier.'

'I told him I'm not going to the party with anyone, but that I'd dance with him when I was there,' Iona told her.

Jinette added a packet of paper hexies to one of the quilt bundle orders. 'Won't you be going with Kier? Surely he'll be back from the city by then.'

Iona shrugged. 'I suppose so, but nothing feels certain. Kier could extend his business trip. That's why it's better if I plan to go without a date. It's your engagement party, and I'm just planning on having a nice time.'

'What about Gairn? You seem to be getting on fine with him. Baking chocolate cake with him last night.' Jinette gave her a knowing smile.

'We're just friends,' Iona insisted. 'The chocolate cake is in the kitchen. He told me to take it for our sewing bee evening tonight.'

'We'll be your tasters. Maybe you have a budding career as a baker or sweetie maker?'

Iona shook her head. 'I'll stick with sewing.'

Text messages were popping up on Jinette's phone. She checked them. 'That's more of the ladies confirming they'll be at the sewing bee tonight for the vintage dresses meeting.'

'I was thinking that some of the floral patterns in our embroidery kits would be great to cover up any small repairs to the dresses.'

'Embroidery is so handy for mending,' Jinette agreed. 'We've got all sorts of flowers, especially ones like the tea roses and violets that fit with vintage themes.'

'The Queen Anne's lace would be perfect too, and the bluebells and pansies.'

'There's a folder with lots of wee flower embroidery designs in the dookit under the counter. We had to cut down on how many designs to make into kits, and all the lovely spare patterns are tucked in the folder.'

Iona reached down and lifted up a folder labelled — floral embroidery designs. 'Here it is.' She put it on the counter and opened it. 'It's packed with patterns.'

'I save all the patterns,' said Jinette. 'You never know when they'll come in handy.'

Iona selected a few, lifting them carefully out of the folder. The names of the flowers were printed on the patterns. 'I love these bellflowers and strawberry flowers. Whose designs are these?'

'Broden, the laird, is an artist. He designed the flower artwork. Eevie and I, and a couple of the ladies from the bee, helped adjust them to make them suitable for embroidering. We'll probably use these when we bring out a new range of embroidery kits.'

'But we can use them?' Iona asked her.

'Yes.' Jinette lifted up one of the designs. 'I've always loved orange blossom.'

'They're certainly appropriate for weddings and brides.'

Jinette looked flustered. 'I keep getting the flutters every time I think that I'm going to be married again. Don't tell Lochty. He'll worry that I'm getting the wedding jitters.'

'I won't tell him. But it's natural to be excited.'

Jinette put the orange blossom back in the folder. 'Keep these at the top of the file. I've a feeling they'll come in handy for the vintage dress work.'

Iona put the orange blossom on top of the bellflowers and strawberry flowers, then tucked the folder under the counter.

For the remainder of the day, Iona and Jinette were kept busy with customers and packing orders. The day flew in.

'Is that the time?' Jinette exclaimed. 'The ladies will be here soon. We'd better get things set up.'

A courier peeped his horn to alert Jinette that he'd come to pick up the shop's orders. He jumped out of his van and opened the rear doors.

'I'll carry the packages out to him,' Iona said to Jinette, making three trips to collect everything.

'A busy day, eh, Iona?' the courier said chirpily, and then jumped in his van, and gave her a cheery wave as he drove off.

It was a different courier from the last time. She shook her head in dismay, and then went back into the shop to help Jinette tidy up and get ready for the sewing bee night.

Neither of them had indulged in a slice of the chocolate cake that Iona had made with Aran, and planned to share it out.

They'd just finished setting up the chairs and tables when the members started to arrive, many of them bringing homemade shortbread, scones and cakes.

Iona looked out the window while Jinette boiled the kettle to make the first large pot of tea. 'Here's Milla — and Aran.'

Jinette hurried through from the kitchen. 'What's Aran doing?'

'It looks like he's carrying two of the boxes filled with vintage dresses. Milla is carrying the other one.'

Jinette wasn't happy. 'I hope he's not thinking of wangling his way into our sewing bee tonight. We're going to be half naked, trying on the vintage dresses. We can't have Aran in the shop.'

'He's not even interested in the vintage dresses, or make do and mend,' Iona told her.

Jinette marched out and took the boxes off him. 'Thanks for helping Milla carry the dresses. We can't wait to try them on.'

He blinked. 'I didn't realise you'd be wearing them tonight. I thought you'd be cutting them up for quilting.' Clearly he had planned on joining them, and Jinette had thwarted him.

Jinette smiled. 'Lovely vintage dresses and a shop full of sewing bee ladies — oh yes, we'll be running around in our unmentionables, so no peeking across at us.'

He looked startled at the mention of this. 'I just thought...I was going to watch Iona hand sewing her quilts. Pick up some tips.'

'Not tonight, Aran,' Jinette said with a smile. 'Another night perhaps.'

He nodded and backed away. 'Yes, some other time when you're not...when you're all wearing your clothes.'

Milla confided to Jinette as Aran headed back to his shop. 'I didn't expect him to grab two of the boxes. I couldn't tell him to fumble off. He was trying to worm his way into the bee.'

'Well,' Jinette said firmly. 'He's not spoiling our fun tonight. This is a night for us girls. If he rethinks his strategy and comes back over later on, we'll get you to strip down to your nifties. That'll stop him.'

Milla gasped. 'I'm not giving him an eyeful of my undies, Jinette.'

By now Jinette was giggling as they carried the boxes into the shop.

Milla sighed with relief and laughed. 'Don't wind me up like that. I thought you were serious.'

'Nah, I was just joking. If we need to resort to underhanded wiles, we'll get Hessie to unbutton her cardigan and show him her black lace basque.'

Hessie was momentarily indignant. 'I should never have confided in you, Jinette. I only wore it once, and it was for a party dress up occasion.'

'A party for two from what I recall. No wonder Tavish wants you as his date for my party.' Jinette winked at the ladies, and tried not to giggle.

Hessie smiled and shook her head at Jinette.

Iona looked at the ladies, the cheery friendships, the welcoming smiles, all helping each other, sharing fabric, patterns and chatter. They'd certainly made her feel welcome, as if she'd been part of the bee for years.

'Okay, Iona,' Jinette announced. 'I'll make the tea, and we'll try the chocolate cake you baked. I've resisted it all day, but now let's have a taste of it.'

'Chocolate cake?' said Airlie. 'Yes, let's get our priorities right. I'll help you set up the tea and plates.'

'I brought a tin of shortbread,' one of the ladies said. She lifted the large tin from her craft bag and set it up on the counter. 'I made it myself.'

Several hands reached in and helped themselves to a shortbread petticoat tail, while Jinette and Airlie sorted the tea.

Iona cut the cake up and put it on a plate.

'The chocolate aroma is scrumptious,' Airlie commented.

'Gairn uses high quality chocolate and cocoa,' Iona explained.

Iona's cake was enjoyed by everyone.

Then after finishing their first round of tea, they began to take the vintage dresses out of the boxes and divide them up into wearable, mendable and upscalable piles.

Milla showed Jinette one of the forties tea dresses. The fabric was pale blue georgette and draped beautifully. 'There's not a mark on this dress. It's hardly been worn. I thought it would fit you. Maybe an idea for your going away dress after your wedding.'

Jinette loved the dress. It had a subtle floral print and a modest sweetheart neckline. 'It's gorgeous.' Jinette held the dress up against herself. 'I hope it fits.'

'Away and try it on,' Milla encouraged her while they rummaged through the other dresses.

Jinette disappeared into the back of the shop with the dress, and emerged again wearing it. She smoothed the fabric down over her waist and hips. 'It feels wonderful, and the fabric is nice.'

Milla checked the fit of the dress on Jinette. 'It's as if it was made for you.'

Jinette nodded and then said, 'What do you think, Iona?'

'It suits you so well, and it would be a classy going away dress. Tea dresses are timeless classics, and the light blue is so summery. Perfect for your wedding ensemble.'

'The fabric is a great match for that blue sapphire dazzler on your finger,' said Hessie.

Jinette admired her engagement ring and then smiled. 'I'd like to keep this dress if it's okay with you, Milla.'

Milla was delighted.

'Are you going away on honeymoon?' one of the ladies asked Jinette.

'I'm fine staying here, but Lochty wants to take me sailing around the isles for a long weekend. Just the two of us. He used to work on the fishing boats when he was a laddie, and he's keen to hire a boat and have us sail off on our honeymoon.'

'The weather should be nice in the summer,' Iona commented.

'The late summertime is a bit unpredictable,' said Jinette. 'But whatever the weather, we'll enjoy ourselves.'

The late summer? Iona frowned. She'd probably have gone home by then.

The conversation focussed again on the dresses, with Milla selecting another dress from a box. 'This tea dress with its vintage rose print is lovely, but it's quite a neat fit. I thought maybe it would suit you, Iona. It's the one you were holding up in my shop.'

Iona accepted the dress, delighted to be given it. 'Thank you, Milla. I love it.'

Hessie nodded. 'It's a very pretty dress. I'll bet it suits you.'

'Try it on,' Jinette encouraged her.

Iona didn't need much encouragement and went through to her bedroom to try it on. It fitted well. She hurried back through, smiling to show the ladies.

'That's definitely the dress for you,' Jinette told Iona. 'Maybe you'll wear it to my party.'

Iona nodded. 'Great idea. I'll do that. I've got a pair of court shoes that'll go with it.'

One of the ladies had her eye on a navy and white polka dot wrap dress. 'I'll buy this one from you, Milla.'

'No, I'm sharing these out for free. I got the dresses as a job lot for very little. I think they just wanted to clear space for new stuff,' Milla explained.

Airlie held up a dress and sighed. 'This one has been well–worn, but I still like it.'

Hessie dug into her sewing bag. 'When I heard about the vintage dresses, I rummaged through my sewing box at home and found these.' It was a pack of three different attachable collars trimmed with lace. 'I bought these a while ago in a sale. A collar sewn on would cover the wear and tear around the neckline.'

Airlie smiled and selected one of the collars. 'I'll buy this one off you, Hessie.'

'No, I brought these to share around,' said Hessie.

Airlie put the dress down on one of the tables and pinned the collar on.

'The machine's set up if you want to sew it on,' Jinette told Airlie.

Airlie stitched the collar on while the others continued to browse through the dresses.

'I think this one has had its day,' said Jinette, looking at another dress. 'We'll put the ones that are only fit for cutting and quilting in one box, and the useable ones in another.'

Iona opened the folder of embroidery patterns. 'We've got embroidery patterns for small floral motifs that could be used to cover any marks.'

'Can I have a copy of that vintage rose?' one of the ladies asked. She'd earmarked a rose print wrap dress. 'There's a rip and a stain on the front that I could hide with a rose embroidery.'

'Help yourselves,' Jinette told them. She lifted a large jar of buttons down from a shelf. 'If there's any buttons missing from the dresses, you'll find plenty to replace them from my spare button jar.'

This idea was another welcome suggestion.

There was a button missing from a dress that Milla wanted to keep, and nothing in the jar matched it.

'Take one of the packets of buttons from the display and replace the old ones with a new set. Just changing the buttons can make a dress look like new,' Jinette advised Milla.

'I'll take these pearl buttons, Jinette,' said Milla, picking a packet of them from the display.

Other members had brought various trims with them in preparation for the vintage dress night.

By the time the ladies had sifted through the dresses, there were more dresses that they were going to mend and upscale than the ones in the box for cutting and quilting.

'That was a great haul, Milla,' Jinette said, smiling. 'We'll have some more tea and then we'll start cutting them up and sharing the fabric.'

Overall, the sewing bee night was a cheerful and lively evening. Iona enjoyed herself and loved the camaraderie and happy atmosphere.

At the end of the night, the ladies left with dresses and fabric for sewing.

Jinette was the last to leave. 'I think we've all done well.' She tucked the dress she'd selected into her sewing bag. 'I'm pleased that you've got a new dress too. Well, an old new dress,' she corrected herself.

'I'll enjoy mending it and embroidering it.' Iona sounded keen to do this.

After everyone left, Iona couldn't resist making a start on mending the dress, and continued stitching well into the night.

The calm and cosy feeling in the shop eased her concerns over Kier. Sewing really was so comforting.

Throughout the next few days, Iona was busy working in the quilt shop, and joined in with the sewing bee nights where the ladies mended and refashioned the vintage dresses.

Several of them had started to make quilts from the remnants of the dresses, and Iona succumbed to stitching a needlebook using pieces of the vintage fabric and adding embroidery.

They'd also celebrated Jinette's birthday, and the sewing bee ladies had clubbed together to buy her a beautiful vintage porcelain tea set, including a teapot, and a birthday cake from the bakery. Lochty bought her the overlocking machine she'd wanted for her dressmaking.

Plans were well underway for the engagement party at the mansion, and Iona was looking forward to wearing her vintage dress and dancing. She'd started making a mini quilt embroidered with Jinette and Lochty's names as an engagement gift that she intended giving to them at the party. She'd also been piecing together a larger quilt as a present for their wedding.

She'd chatted to Gairn when buying bread and cakes from the bakers, but had seen very little of Aran. He'd waved to her from the sewing shop window and indicated that he was up to his eyeballs in quilt orders. Few local customers went into his shop, at least that's the impression she had. From the window of the quilt shop she'd seen that his shop was usually empty, except for him working away at his sewing machine. But Jinette's shop had been busy with customers buying the new fabric ranges and embroidery kits.

One lunchtime, Iona borrowed Jinette's bicycle that was kept in the shop's garden shed, and cycled up to the loch. It was an old–fashioned bicycle, painted pale blue and it had a basket on the front. Jinette often filled the basket with flowers and used it as a prop for the photographs of the quilts that were posted up on the shop's website. It created a pretty vintage look.

Iona cycled past Kier's estate and felt a tinge of sadness when she saw his farmhouse in the distance. Apparently, he was still in the city on business, and had extended his stay.

She sat on a heather bed and ate her packed lunch while looking out over the loch, remembering the smiles and laughter she'd shared with Kier.

It was as if her life had settled into what she'd expected when she'd first started work at the quilt shop. No romance, just working with all the pretty fabric, making quilts and enjoying the summer.

Finishing her lunch, she cycled along the road and tried not to look at Kier's farmhouse or his fields as she headed towards the village. The sewing bee was on that night and she planned to bake scones for the ladies.

CHAPTER ELEVEN

The sewing bee night was busy. It was the evening before Jinette's engagement party and the atmosphere buzzed with excitement.

Several members finished mending their vintage dresses and it was like a dress rehearsal — all helping each other to decide if their dresses looked suitable for the party.

Iona wore the dress she'd mended with motifs of floral embroidery. She stood on a chair and twirled around slowly while Milla checked that the hemline was even.

'Yes,' Milla told her. 'You've made a neat job of the hem. It's a good length for you.'

'I thought I'd wear this for the party.' Jinette held up a dark blue silk dress. 'I made this and I've never worn it. It's a vintage pattern and I love the full skirt.'

Iona stepped down from the chair. 'It's a beautiful dress, Jinette.'

'It'll be lovely for dancing in,' added Hessie.

'With most of us wearing vintage style dresses, it's going to look like a theme for the party,' said Jinette.

'You'll need to take loads of pictures,' Milla told her. 'You can put them up on your website to show people what can be done with a bit of make do and mend, or stitching new dresses from vintage patterns.'

Jinette nodded. 'I'll do that.' She glanced at the shelves of fabric. 'I'll make sure I have suitable fabric in stock, and a few more vintage dress patterns. The classics are always popular. The pattern I used for my dress is one I've had for years. It's easy to make, no wee fiddly bits, and although the skirt has some swish, it doesn't take as much fabric as you'd think to make it.'

'You should definitely encourage customers to consider the floral embroidery for covering marks on dresses,' one of the ladies remarked.

'Or just to add an embroidered flower on clothes,' said Airlie.

'I will,' Jinette said, nodding. 'Iona suggested we add a set of flower patterns to our embroidery kits. Wee flowers, like a rose, daisy, bluebell, pansy, that sort of pretty flower. They're perfect for sewing on to a dress or top as a motif.'

'I'll put the kettle on for our tea,' Iona said, heading through to her bedroom to change out of the vintage dress and into her regular clothes.

'Remember, we're have a champagne tea,' Jinette announced.

The ladies smiled and got everything set up. Most of them had brought cakes or scones.

Iona busied herself in the kitchen. She'd made champagne cupcakes as well as scones. She carried a cake stand through and sat it on the shop counter. The cupcakes were topped with white and pink champagne buttercream.

Jinette carried through two bottles of champagne, and a couple of the ladies had also brought bottles of bubbly to celebrate Jinette's engagement.

'We're going to be tipsy tonight,' Hessie remarked, helping set up the glasses and cups.

'We'll be tipsy tomorrow night no doubt,' said Jinette, 'but I wanted us to celebrate at the bee this evening.' She popped open one of the bottles and poured the bubbly into the glasses as the tea was served up too.

They drank toasts, shared the champagne, enjoyed the cakes and scones, and chatted happily.

'Have you heard from Kier?' Airlie asked Iona.

'Not a word,' Iona replied.

'Lochty's been working in Kier's flower fields,' Jinette told them. 'He's heard that Kier is still in the city on business. Kier's been away for a few weeks in the past.'

'Surely he'll try to be back for your party,' Hessie remarked.

Jinette shrugged. 'I don't know.' She didn't want to say too much so as not to upset Iona.

'Have you heard anything else?' Iona asked her, sensing she was holding back on some gossip. 'I'm fine about him not contacting me.'

Hessie shook her head in disapproval. 'Men can be such fools at times. It doesn't always mean they don't care. They're just eejits when it comes to romance.'

Jinette glanced at Iona, sighed and then said. 'I've heard that he was in touch with Margeaux. But nothing that suggested they were dating.'

Iona's heart felt crushed, but she hid her reaction behind a smile. 'I'm not wrapping my hopes and dreams around Kier.'

Jinette sensed the hurt behind the smile. 'Lochty thinks that Kier could be replacing Margeaux's company with a different one.'

'Perhaps he is,' said Iona. 'But that's his business.'

'Aran's been keeping himself to himself,' Hessie said, glancing over at the sewing shop.

Iona nodded. 'He has. He waves in the morning, and then gets on with his work.'

'I've seen him working away at his sewing machine,' Milla told them. 'He's up early and works late. It's quilts he's been stitching. I've seen him whizzing them through his machine. But he still hasn't had many local customers.'

'He'll make a fair profit from his online sales,' Jinette commented.

'Maybe when he's cleared his orders he'll be more sociable,' said Airlie.

'Is Aran still coming to your party?' one of the ladies asked Jinette.

'I think so. He said he was coming along,' Jinette replied. 'Gairn's definitely going. I spoke to him this morning when I bought my bread from the bakers.'

'There will be plenty of men for you to dance with, Iona,' said Hessie.

'Yes, I'll be up dancing. I'm looking forward to the party,' Iona confirmed.

'Lochty says he's going to burl you around the dance floor.' Jinette smiled at Iona. 'So you've been warned.'

Iona laughed.

'You can laugh,' said Jinette, 'but he's an enthusiastic dancer. He'll lift you off your feet.'

'Sounds like fun.' Iona smiled, determined that she would enjoy herself.

'Maybe Iona will outdance your Lochty,' Hessie suggested to Jinette.

'I'll be ready to take pictures of that fiasco,' Jinette joked.

The lighthearted conversation eased Iona's hurt at missing Kier, and feeling angry with herself for letting her feelings for him get the better of her.

111

'Will the laird be back for the party?' Airlie asked Jinette.

'No, Broden left a message for Lochty saying he won't be there, but he's had his staff at the mansion get ready to lay on a lavish buffet for us.' Jinette smiled. 'But he'll definitely be at our wedding. And we'll be having our reception at the mansion.'

'Have you decided on a date yet?' one of the ladies asked Jinette.

'No firm date, but we should have one soon,' Jinette confirmed. 'It's such an exciting time.'

Iona smiled, pleased for Jinette, and happy that she felt part of everything.

At the end of the sewing bee night, the ladies filtered out, chatting cheerfully, looking forward to the engagement party.

Iona waved them off and locked the shop door. The lights were on in the sewing shop and the bakery. No doubt she'd dance with Gairn and Aran at the party, but whether Kier would be back remained to be seen.

The main street seemed extra busy the following day and there was a sense of excitement in the air. The local hairdresser was kept busy styling the ladies hair for the party. Jinette had booked to have her hair done in the afternoon. Iona manned the quilt shop on her own for most of the working day to allow Jinette to flit about preparing for the night.

Iona closed the shop at the end of the day and started to get ready for the party. She washed and styled her own hair, brushing it smooth, and pinning the sides up with diamanté clasps.

Stepping into her court shoes, she shrugged on a light jacket over her vintage dress, and picked up her bag and the mini quilt she'd gift wrapped for Jinette and Lochty.

It was a warm summer evening, and she walked the short distance up the main street to the mansion. She'd seen it on passing, but this was the first time she'd been inside.

Sounds of the party filtered out the front entrance and into the night air as Iona walked up to the front door. The door was open wide, and she heard music playing in the background. Hotel staff were busy attending to the guests, and as she stepped inside she was greeted by Tavish. He was similar in age to Lochty, and wore a staff badge with his name on it. She'd never met him before, but he recognised her and smiled.

'Come away in, Iona. I'll take your jacket for you.'

Handing him her jacket, Iona then followed him into the hub of the party.

'The party's through here. Help yourself to the buffet and sit wherever suits you.' He indicated over to a long table where Jinette and Lochty were seated. Hessie, Airlie, Milla and other members of the sewing bee were seated at two of the tables next to it.

Jinette smiled and waved at Iona. 'We've kept you a seat.'

Iona realised she was to be seated next to Jinette.

'This is just a wee minding for your engagement.' Iona handed the gift to Jinette and smiled at her and Lochty. He'd spruced himself up again, beard trimmed, and wore a smart suit.

'Thank you, Iona.' Jinette and Lochty were delighted to see that she'd stitched their names on to the mini quilt, something they could keep forever as a marker of their engagement.

Lochty smiled at Iona. 'We'll hang it up on our wall. I like the colours. Very thoughtful of you.'

Gifts, chatter and other guests arriving created a happy atmosphere, and Iona couldn't remember the last time she'd felt part of something like this.

An announcement was made by Tavish. 'On behalf of everyone here at the mansion, and all the guests, we'd like to congratulate Jinette and Lochty on their engagement, wish them all the luck in the world, and ask them to take to the dance floor for the first dance of the evening.'

Everyone cheered and applauded as Jinette and Lochty started dancing. Jinette looked lovely in her new dress, and Iona admitted that they looked like a well–matched couple.

Tavish hurried over to Hessie. 'That's me finished my shift. I'll go and change my clothes and be right back.'

'Tavish had to work tonight getting the party ready,' Hessie explained to Iona.

'He seems very nice.'

'Yes, he is.'

Seated at a table nearby was Gairn, along with his father and other friends. He nodded to Iona and she smiled back at him. Moments later he came over and held out his hand. 'Would you care to dance, Iona?'

She stood up and accompanied him on to the dance floor.

'You look beautiful this evening,' Gairn complimented her. 'Is that one of the vintage dresses that everyone's been talking about?'

'It is. Milla shared the dresses out and I was lucky enough to get this one.'

'It suits you.'

She smiled and thought how handsome Gairn looked in his suit. She'd only seen him in his bakery whites, and seeing him in a smart charcoal suit, white shirt and tie, made her realise how handsome he was.

Gairn was an adept dancer too, but she kept in step with him, and felt at ease as they danced around the floor.

She noticed Aran had arrived and was standing at the side of the bar watching her dancing with Gairn. As she whirled around the floor to the lively music, she glanced at him and he nodded at her. She smiled and continued dancing with Gairn.

After a couple of dances, Gairn accompanied her to the buffet that was set up at the side of the room. A lavish array of food was displayed on long tables and staff were on hand to help serve the food and drink.

'This looks delicious,' Iona said to Gairn. 'I didn't have dinner.'

'Neither did I,' Gairn said, helping himself to the fresh salmon and a selection of vegetables and salad.

Iona opted for a pasta dish.

They sat down at one of the tables and staff brought them tea. Iona had barely tasted her food when Aran came over to talk to her.

'Vintage suits you,' Aran told her, admiring her dress.

She smiled up at him. 'Thank you. How are you getting on with your sewing shop? You seem to have been very busy.'

'A busy bee,' he said chirpily. 'A ton of quilt orders. I'm sorry I haven't had time to pop over to see you at the shop, but I've been working crazy hours.' He glanced at Gairn. 'Almost as many hours as Gairn, though I'm not up quite so early as his five–thirty morning starts.'

Gairn shrugged. 'A baker's life. An early start. I'm only working into the night because of the chocolate work I'm doing. When I'm back here in the autumn, I plan on having most of my evenings free to relax and enjoy myself.'

Aran smiled. 'Well, you're here enjoying yourself this evening, dining and dancing with Iona.' The jealous tone in Aran's voice was unmistakable. 'Hopefully, you'll save a dance for me later on, Iona.'

'I certainly will,' she confirmed.

'I'll let you both get on with your dinner.' Aran then left them alone.

'That felt tense, or am I reading too much into Aran's attitude?' Gairn asked Iona.

'No, he's quite an intense man, even though he's seemingly very relaxed.'

'And secretive.'

'Is there something I should know?'

Gairn nodded. 'Probably, but I can't tell you what it is.'

'Why not?'

'Because I don't know what he's up to.'

'You suspect he's up to something?'

'Yes, his routine at the shop is full–on. He's sewing from morning until night. As if he has a deadline for his quilt orders.'

'Maybe he's just busy,' she suggested.

'He's certainly busy, but it's the unsettled feeling that makes me unsettled too.' He shook the notion away and told her, 'My father and I have made a start on converting the upstairs of the bakery shop.'

'To make it into a tea shop?'

He nodded. 'When we stripped back everything, there's more room upstairs than we first thought. So it'll be perfect for the tea shop. I wish I didn't have to go back to the city to finish my training and could just get stuck in here, working with my father.'

Iona looked over at Gairn's father. He was with friends and having a good time.

'I'm sure the time will whiz in,' she said.

'What about you? Any further plans to stay here?'

She shook her head and tried to smile. 'No plans.'

He paused and then mentioned Kier. 'I hear that Kier is still in the city, working on business matters.'

'According to Lochty, he is.'

'Have you heard from Kier?'

She shook her head and sipped her tea.

Gairn didn't pry any more.

After their food, they took to the dance floor again. During one slower dance, Iona felt a tap on her shoulder and turned to see Lochty standing there smiling.

'I believe you said that you can outdance me, Iona.'

'Eh, no...I didn't—'

'Excuse me while I cut–in,' Lochty said to Gairn, and then whirled Iona around the dance floor, causing Jinette and others to clap and cheer them on.

Iona wasn't sure if she'd outdanced Lochty. But she felt well twirled and in need of sitting down and having a cold drink.

While she sipped her drink, a voice said over her shoulder. 'Will you dance with me?'

She glanced round and saw Aran standing there, holding his hand out, ready to lead her on to the dance floor.

Throughout the evening Iona danced with Gairn, Aran, Lochty and a couple of other men. She had a great time. She even danced with Tavish. He'd asked Iona for a waltz around the floor.

Iona loved the dancing and getting to know other people from the village.

Later, she was standing getting some fresh air near the patio doors. The doors were open to let the cool air drift in. The scent of the mansion's garden was wonderful, and Jinette pointed out the winterhouse that was situated further down the garden.

'That's the winterhouse. The mansion's garden looks beautiful in the wintertime.'

'Kier mentioned that he was building a summerhouse because he admired the laird's winterhouse,' Iona told her. 'But then he said it wasn't quite a summerhouse, so I suggested he call it an autumnhouse.'

'So you're the one responsible for naming it the autumnhouse,' Lochty said, overhearing the conversation.

'Sort of,' Iona said to Lochty.

'Kier's been talking about it when phoning the man in charge of the fields while he's away,' Lochty told Iona. 'Kier wants the building work to continue, and one of the joiners has been adding the windows and the roof.'

'I suppose it's looking good,' she surmised.

Lochty nodded. 'When it's finished I'm sure it'll rival Broden's winterhouse for its beautiful design.'

'I love the autumn,' Jinette remarked.

'I love the summer and the winter,' said Iona. 'Kier says he loves the winter season.'

'I'd have thought the spring and summer would be his seasons,' Jinette remarked.

Iona agreed. 'But he said that his fields have a stark beauty in the wintertime. He made it sound perfect.'

'It is perfect,' a man's voice said over Iona's shoulder.

She recognised the voice immediately. 'Kier. You're back!'

Her heart ached when she saw him standing there looking so tall and handsome. He was dressed in an expensive business suit, white shirt and silk tie. His blond hair made her want to run her fingers through it, to push it back from his troubled brow. He was frowning, wondering what her reaction would be to seeing him again.

'Oh, they're playing our song,' Jinette said to Lochty.

'Are they?' Lochty seemed hesitant.

Jinette smiled tightly at him.

'So they are,' Lochty agreed, getting the message. 'I didn't recognise it at first. Come on, Jinette. Let's have a wee burl.' He waltzed her off, tactfully leaving Iona and Kier to talk.

'I know I have some explaining to do,' Kier began. He gestured outside to the garden. 'Want to get some fresh air?'

Iona let him lead her outside into the warm summer night. Everyone was inside the mansion, so they had the garden all to themselves. The garden extended all the way down to the winterhouse and was bordered by trees. The air smelled of night–scented stock and other flowers.

He stopped before they reached the winterhouse and gazed down at her. His beautiful grey eyes were filled with concern. 'I don't know where to begin.'

'You've been away for longer than you intended,' she said.

'I wanted to contact you, but I didn't want to lie.'

'Why would you need to lie?'

'If you'd asked me about certain things, I wouldn't have been able to give you an answer. There are things that happened, unexpected events, that required my discretion. Things I couldn't tell you because I couldn't risk it becoming gossip.'

'I wouldn't have told anyone.'

'When I explain, you'll understand that it would've been difficult for you to keep the news a secret, especially from Jinette and the ladies at the sewing bee. You all confide in each other.'

'What news? Why is it a secret?'

'Legally, I needed to keep it to myself until the issue was officially confirmed.'

'I still don't know what you're talking about.'

'I can tell you now, but hear me out before you jump to the wrong conclusion.'

She nodded. 'Okay.'

'Everything went according to plan when I arrived in the city. I met with Margeaux and the man who is the head of the company she works for. I was never alone with her, except for a few brief moments when I made it clear that I'm not interested in dating her.'

'So what happened to keep you in the city?'

'I was planning to drive home when my lawyer contacted me. Broden and I, as you know, are benefactors for the local community. We're informed if properties are put on the market for sale. There aren't that many farmhouses or cottages available to buy, so when one is put on the market, our lawyers keep us updated. Whether it's a house or one of the businesses in the main street. Many of them are converted cottages, like Jinette's quilt shop.'

'Does this have anything to do with Jinette's shop?'

He shook his head. 'No, but when I saw the property that had just been put on the market for a quick sale, I had to do something about it. I phoned Broden and we discussed buying it between the two of us, but then I decided to buy it outright.'

'What property was it?'

'The sewing shop.'

Iona blinked. 'The sewing shop? Aran put it up for a quick sale?'

Kier nodded. 'I was as surprised as you clearly are. Aran is a secretive one. But he didn't know that I'm alerted to any property sales in the village.'

'Why is he selling the shop?'

'He's moving back to Edinburgh. His property agent has continued scouting for ideal shop premises for him, and one is now available in the exact area that he'd originally wanted to set up his business. It has accommodation that he can live in too.'

'So, Aran's leaving? You're sure?'

'Yes, but I had to wait until I knew the deal had gone through before telling you. There were issues with paperwork, but it's settled now.'

'The sewing shop has been sold?' It didn't seem quite real. And Kier was right. She would've found it difficult to keep this information to herself. She'd probably have confided in Jinette and soon it would've been the topic of local gossip.

'Yes, I've bought it outright. It was a bargain for a quick sale. Aran wants to move away and start up the new shop in Edinburgh right away.'

'Will you offer the sewing shop property to Gairn and his father?'

'I phoned them. They're not interested in the sewing shop now. They're keen to extend and convert their bakery premises. It'll be more economical, and I agree that it's the best idea for them.'

'So what will happen to the sewing shop?'

'I'll keep it as a going concern during the summer, until I decide what I'll do with it.'

Kier gave her a lingering look. 'I'll need someone to run the shop.'

Her heart fluttered. 'I wonder where you'll find them?'

'I'm looking at her.'

She smiled, and didn't know what to say.

'If you don't want to run the sewing shop, it's okay.'

'When does Aran plan to move away?'

'Apparently, not for a few weeks yet. But when he does, and if you don't want to run the sewing shop, I'll close it until Broden gets back and we'll decide what to do with it.'

Iona nodded, glad that she had time to plan what she'd do. She definitely wanted to run the sewing shop.

'You could obviously live in the cottage at the back of the sewing shop, rather like you do at the quilt shop. It would allow you to stay here longer, to have somewhere to live when Eevie comes back to her old job with Jinette.'

'I'd be here for Jinette's wedding.'

'You would. And maybe we could have a fresh start, without the pressure of you having to move away so soon. We'd have a chance to get to know each other, while you'd have your own shop to run.'

'I love that idea, but it wouldn't be my shop.'

'It would if you wanted it. We could arrange something. Even if I rented the premises to you, the business would still be yours.'

'I have no money to start up a business. I'd need to buy stock. I couldn't afford it.'

'Yes you could. I'd invest in the business. The money would let you buy the stock you needed.'

'No strings attached?'

'None. It would help clear up the mess, the chaos that Aran has caused. Jinette wouldn't be concerned about having a rival. If there's one person she knows she could trust to run the sewing shop fairly, it would be you. Both your shops could benefit.'

'When will Jinette find out about this?'

'Tomorrow. I wanted her to enjoy her party without this muddying the party atmosphere. So don't tell Jinette or Lochty.'

'I won't,' Iona promised.

Kier gazed at her. 'I've missed you.'

'I've missed you too.'

'Want to dance? Everyone will be wondering what we're up to out here.'

She smiled and nodded, and walked with him back up to the mansion where they had their first dance.

She'd enjoyed dancing with Gairn. Laughed when dancing with Lochty. And didn't feel in step with Aran. But when she danced with Kier, it felt so right. Everything felt right again in her world now that Kier was home.

CHAPTER TWELVE

Jinette and Lochty's engagement party was a great success. At the end of the evening Iona collected her jacket and got ready to leave.

'Can I drive you back to the quilt shop?' Kier asked her.

Iona smiled at him. 'Yes, I'd like that.'

Kier escorted her outside. The night air was a heady blend of greenery from the trees in the mansion's driveway, and the warmth of a summer evening.

His car was parked in front of the mansion, and Iona got in and immediately felt at ease, as if she was where she belonged.

Kier's tall stature and manly presence filled the car when he got in and started it up. He drove them away, down the main street and parked outside the quilt shop. He didn't turn the engine off as he didn't want to pressure her into inviting him in, as he thought that would inevitably lead to fighting the urge to take her in his arms and kiss her — to tell her how much he'd missed her, and that he was glad she'd welcomed him back into her life.

'I had a great time dancing with you, Kier. But I think I'm all danced out, and as I'm working in the morning, I should get straight to bed.'

He raised his eyebrows and smiled wickedly.

She blushed and laughed. 'On my own,' she scolded him.

He nodded and smiled at her. Such a sexy smile that made her almost change her mind and invite him in. But she didn't.

'I'll see you in the morning no doubt,' he said. He had flower deliveries to do. Despite being rich and capable of hiring others to make the deliveries, he'd always enjoyed the early mornings and dropping in on various shops, chatting to the owners.

Iona nodded. 'See you in the morning.'

He waited until she'd gone inside and then drove off, turning the car around and driving off up the main street, heading home.

She gazed out the window, watching the tail lights of his car disappear into the night, and then got ready for bed.

Kier lay awake in his bedroom wondering what to do. He'd missed Iona when he'd been in the city, and now he was back, he was missing her even more. She'd looked beautiful at the party, and her warm nature made him miss her company.

He checked the time. Almost dawn. He'd be up soon to attend to the fields, gather the fresh flowers for the deliveries, and get the day started. He closed his eyes and tried to catch a handful of hours sleep before he had to get up again.

Iona surprised herself by bouncing out of bed minutes before her alarm went off. Her eagerness to get up, shower, dress and get ready to open the shop was unexpected. She'd thought that with all the late night dancing and excitement, she'd have hidden under the patchwork quilt when it was time to get up.

Taking advantage of her energetic attitude, she tidied herself, ate cereal and fruit for breakfast, and then opened the front door of the shop, letting the warm summer morning shine in.

She blinked against a band of sunlight glinting off the sewing shop window. At first she thought it was the dazzle that had made it look like the front window was empty. She blinked again. No, it was empty. Was Aran changing out his entire display? Surely he wouldn't remove the pretty pink sewing machine or the decorative bunting.

As the sun faded for a moment behind a cloud, she saw clearly that the shop was empty, and there was a notice in the window.

Her heart jolted. Why was the shop empty? Kier said that Aran wasn't leaving for weeks.

Grabbing the shop keys, she locked the door and ran across to the sewing shop.

She cupped her hands and peered through the window. The shop was in darkness, and the bright sunshine glinted off the window, making it difficult to see inside. But she was sure it was empty. Nothing was left in the window display. No dress mannequin, no quilts, fabric...no sign that Aran had ever been there.

It was the strangest feeling. Aran must've done a moonlight flit. He'd obviously packed up everything into his van during the depths of the night and left without a word to anyone. She'd slept through it, not hearing a sound. She didn't know how to feel. Sad, deceived, relieved, happy? A little bit of all of that.

Before she could contemplate this, she saw Jinette walking down the road from her cottage. From her cheerful wave and smile, Jinette had no idea what had happened.

'Jinette, look, the sewing shop is empty,' Iona called to her.

Jinette's smile faded and she hurried up to see what was going on.

'Aran's gone. He's done a moonlight flit,' Iona told her.

'What?' Jinette exclaimed. It was more of a surprise for her because Iona hadn't had a chance to tell her about Aran putting the sewing shop up for a quick sale.

Jinette tried the door. 'It's locked.' She read the closed sign. 'Is that it? He's gone. Puff. And he's away?'

'Kier confided in me last night at the party,' Iona began. 'It's the reason he extended his trip to the city.' Iona summarised the details. 'Kier was going to tell you this morning. He didn't want to tell you last night so as not to spoil your party. He thought that Aran was staying on for weeks, so it seemed like there was no rush to let you know.'

Jinette nodded. 'I understand. That was thoughtful of Kier, and you.' She glared at the empty shop. 'But Aran could've said something. If he had the chance of his dream shop in Edinburgh, fine, we'd have wished him all the luck. But to disappear without a word.' She shook her head. 'That means he must have been with us last night at the party, knowing full well he was going to leave immediately. He looked us all in the eye and never said a thing.'

Iona agreed. 'There's nothing we can do, so please don't let it spoil your day.'

Jinette put her hand on Iona's arm. 'Thank you, Iona. I won't.'

They were peering through the window when Kier drove up. He jumped out of the car. 'Has he gone? Is it true? The keys to the shop were dropped off at my house with a brief note saying he was leaving right away to open his new shop in Edinburgh.' He bit his lip, keeping his comments to himself. There was no use getting angry with Aran. He was gone.

'He seems to have taken everything,' said Jinette. 'He must have loaded it into his van at two or three in the morning while everyone was asleep. In a town that gossips, he's managed to disappear in secret. Just like he set up his shop.'

123

Kier used the keys to unlock the front door. 'Come on in, let's see if there's anything left.'

The three of them went into the shop. Kier flicked the lights on, but it wasn't necessary because the sun brightened the sewing shop.

At first glance, the shop looked bare. Nothing on the counter. Bare shelves and empty cupboards.

Then Kier looked up to one of the high shelves where the wedding satin fabric had been kept out of the way from constant handling. He reached up and pulled down a full roll of the wedding fabric that had been earmarked for Jinette.

'Jinette's wedding dress fabric,' said Iona. 'It's the only thing he's left.'

Kier put the roll of fabric on the clean counter.

Jinette checked it. 'Not even a note. Obviously he's left this for me.'

'What do you want to do?' Iona asked her.

Jinette hooked her sewing bag on to her arm and lifted up the roll of fabric, claiming it as her own. 'I'll take it, thank you.'

Iona and Kier smiled.

'I'll leave you two to talk things over,' Jinette said, 'while I run off to the shop with my treasure.'

The lighthearted tone helped ease the shock that Aran had gone as Iona stood in the centre of the empty premises.

Iona turned around slowly, remembering how pretty the shop had looked when filled with fabric, bright lights and the whirring sewing machine — and now picturing what it could look like, the possibilities if she took on the challenge. A temporary challenge during the summer until it was time to go home.

'What will you do now?' she said to Kier, finally pausing in front of him.

He dangled the shop keys.

She sighed heavily. 'I wanted time to consider things. It's quite a challenge taking on a new shop.'

He continued dangling the keys. 'I have every confidence in you. But if it doesn't work out, hand the keys back to me.'

'You make it sound so easy.'

'Nothing in business is ever easy. But you're a hard worker, reliable, and Jinette has confided in me that she couldn't have asked for a better assistant for the summer.'

Iona accepted the keys to the sewing shop.

Kier smiled at her. 'If you change your mind, speak up. I'll understand.'

Knowing that she had an option to back out of the agreement made her feel better.

'Can I have a look at the accommodation at the back?' she asked.

'You're the boss now, Iona.' He gestured for her to lead the way through to the living room.

She glanced around, picturing how cosy it would be at night. Similar to the quilt shop accommodation, it had a living room, small kitchen and bathroom, and a bedroom that had a view of the back garden.

She opened one of the cupboards in the hallway and found that it was stuffed with lots of pretty vintage items — including lamps, ornaments, old–fashioned candle lights, and vintage floral cushions.

'Aran must've stashed these away in the cupboards,' she said. 'He wasn't a lover of vintage.' She lifted out one of the lamps and set it down on a dresser in the living room.

'I'll have everything thoroughly cleaned for you moving in.'

'I could clean it.'

'No, you've enough work to do at the quilt shop. I'll sort this out for you. A new mattress for the bed, new linen.' He listed off the essentials he'd replace.

She smiled at him.

'Hello, there?' a voice called through to them.

They went back through to the shop.

'The door was open,' Gairn said, looking around at the bare bones of the shop. 'What's happened? Has Aran left early? I know it was a quick sale, but I thought he was working here for several more weeks.'

Kier shrugged. 'Aran packed up during the night.'

Gairn frowned. 'No warning? No explanation?'

'Nope.' Kier told him the details.

Gairn shook his head in dismay.

'Iona is taking over the running of the sewing shop,' Kier explained.

Gairn smiled. 'Permanently I hope.'

'I'm not sure. But I'll be here for the whole summer, even if Eevie comes back early. I'll be living here, so Eevie can live again in the quilt shop.'

Gairn continued to smile. 'Maybe you'll fall in love with the sewing shop and never want to leave.'

Iona's heart fluttered with excitement at the thought of staying. Now she had the sewing shop and somewhere to live. The pressure of having to leave lifted.

Gairn sounded chirpy. 'Well, I'd better get the cakes out of the oven. Another busy day. See you later.' And off he bounded, clearly pleased with the outcome.

'Gairn really didn't want this shop then,' she said to Kier.

'No, Gairn and his father have found out that extending their own premises is ideal for them. So you'll have a cheerful neighbour.'

Iona smiled. 'Well, I'd better go and help Jinette with the orders. A busy day.'

They stepped outside the sewing shop. Iona locked the door and handed the keys to Kier.

He frowned.

'You'll need them if you're going to have the premises cleaned,' she explained.

His frown lifted. 'For a moment, I thought you'd changed your mind.'

'No, I haven't. In fact, I'm already planning the fabric you're going to buy for the stock.' She laughed, teasing him.

He smiled at her. 'Email me a list of all the fabric and stock you'll need to get the shop up and running.'

'I will,' she assured him. 'After work, I'll start searching through the websites that Jinette uses to find the fabrics I want. Ones that won't clash with hers. If you see the lights burning in the quilt shop tonight, it'll be me burning the midnight oil making lists of fabric, thread and trims.'

She sounded so enthusiastic, and he hid his partial disappointment behind a smile.

Waving cheerfully, she hurried over to the quilt shop, leaving him wondering what to do. He'd planned to ask her to have dinner with him. But now, it would put her in an awkward position, unable to say no due to him effectively handing her the sewing shop.

He walked back to his car with a heavy heart. He would never want Iona to feel obliged to have dinner with him, to date him. He'd have to remain friends with her. Friends with potential, but nothing more. The last thing he wanted was a relationship built on wrong assumptions. He'd aimed to take things slowly with Iona, so as not to hurt her. He knew he wouldn't deliberately hurt her, for he saw a glimmer of a future together with her. Now he'd have to slow things even further, keeping things light and friendly.

Iona's day at the quilt shop was a busy one. There were orders to pack, customers to deal with in the shop, but also a stream of people popping in, mainly the sewing bee ladies, to gossip about Aran leaving the sewing shop in the depths of the night. The drama was the talk of the village.

Finally, Jinette picked up her bag ready to go home for the night. 'Are you seeing Kier this evening?'

'No, I'm going to make my dinner and then scour those websites you showed me to select the fabrics for the shop,' Iona explained.

Jinette frowned. 'I thought you'd be having dinner with him at his house. With him being away for a while, and now back. The two of you seemed to be getting on well last night. Dancing, sneaking off into the garden for a wee canoodle.'

Iona laughed. 'There was no canoodling. Just talking about what he'd been up to when he was away.'

'So, Margeaux is definitely off the scene?'

Iona nodded firmly. 'She is. Kier won't be dealing with her, or the company she works for, ever again. He's found another company to deal with.'

'I'm glad, but I still thought the pair of you were on the verge of being a proper couple.'

'No, we're taking things slowly.'

Jinette hoisted her sewing bag on to her shoulder. 'I'll see you in the morning.'

'Yes. Have a nice evening with Lochty.'

Jinette paused and looked at Iona. 'Thank you for assuring me that you'll continue being my assistant until Eevie comes back, even when you've got the sewing shop.'

'I wouldn't leave you in the lurch. We'll share the work and help each other.'

'I'll help you with the sewing shop too, and so will the sewing bee ladies,' said Jinette.

Waving happily, Jinette headed home.

Iona locked the shop for the night, popped a pizza in the oven for her dinner, and started to scour the web for fabric.

Remnants of the pizza were lying on her plate beside the computer. She drank her tea and focussed on the wonderful array of fabrics available. The night flew in, and she did end up burning the midnight oil, before flicking the computer off and going to bed.

Kier had been busy too. He'd caught up on business, and then arranged for the woman who cleaned his house to clean the sewing shop.

He kept checking his emails to see if there was one from Iona with a list of fabrics attached, but there was nothing. He assumed she was sitting at the computer in the quilt shop scrolling through the different fabrics she'd need to stock the sewing shop.

During the following week, the sewing shop was restocked with a wonderful selection of fabric, thread and trims. Jinette and the ladies of the sewing bee helped Iona set it up, with everyone excited to pitch in to help. Ultimately, they'd all benefit from having lots of new fabric for their sewing and quilting.

The accommodation was cleaned, and new bedding and other items added, and the vintage items from the cupboard were put back where they could be used and admired. The vintage lamps gave a warm glow to the living room, as did the candle lantern in the bedroom. The kitchen looked quaint and had been stocked with food, including a full freezer.

Kier and Iona saw each other or were in contact almost every day, and yet, he continued to hesitate when it came to asking her to have dinner with him.

The opening of the sewing shop was a fun day, with the local community happy to support Iona's new venture. Kier had supplied the hanging baskets of flowers for the outside of the shop, and a gardenia tree.

Iona had set up an online store and was already getting orders.

Kier invested in buying everything Iona needed including a fantastic new sewing machine. Despite loving her hand quilting, there were other things that the sewing machine was ideal for making. Her online sales were starting to pick up, and she couldn't remember when she'd felt so happy. Her friendship with Kier was strong, but she'd held back on taking things to the next level. Sometimes, she saw the look in his eyes, as if he wanted to ask her out on a date, and then he'd smile, joke with her, and the moment was gone.

After busy days flitting between helping Jinette and running the sewing shop, Iona enjoyed the comfort of the cottage accommodation. In the evenings she often continue working on tasks needed for the sewing shop, but also relaxed in the living room by the glow of the vintage lamps, finishing her patchwork quilt. Hand stitching it helped her unwind.

Baking scones and cakes was another pleasure, and she'd picked up tips for making her scones lighter and fluffier from Gairn when he popped in to see her for tea and a chat. He'd asked her if she'd sew the curtains for the tea shop and other items for a vintage look. She'd selected the old–fashioned tea rose fabric, but was waiting until all the building work was finished so that she could get an exact measurement of the windows. Huge progress had been made on the conversion because Gairn wanted it finished soon so he could make plans for when he came back to work there.

Nothing was officially settled about Iona staying in the sewing shop permanently, but as each day went by, she started to feel like she would settle in the village and wouldn't go back to her old flat.

One hot summer evening Kier was working in his garden, building the autumnhouse. He'd almost finished it. Building it in the evenings occupied his time while Iona continued to occupy his thoughts.

The warm summer sunlight made everything look like burnished gold in the early evening.

Lochty approached Kier. 'Can I have a word with you?'

Kier stopped working on the autumnhouse and nodded. 'Yes.'

Lochty sighed. 'I know it's none of my business, but I'm worried about you and Iona.'

'Worried? Why?'

'It's obvious the two of you like each other as more than friends. I've seen the way you look at her.'

Kier didn't deny it.

Lochty continued. 'I know you have your reasons, because she's got the sewing shop and all that, but don't make the same mistake that I made with Jinette when I was a young man like you. I've only ever loved Jinette, but I dragged my heels when I was young, and I let her slip through my fingers. Another man, bolder than me, asked her to marry him. It should've been me, not him. I'm going to marry her now, but...'

'I understand. And it's been on my mind too.' He ran a frustrated hand through his thick blond hair that the sun had lightened while giving him a golden tan.

'You need to tell Iona how you really feel about her. That you love her.'

Kier didn't deny this either.

'Don't make the mistake that I made,' Lochty emphasised. 'I wasted a lot of years because of it.'

Kier nodded.

Lochty then walked away.

Kier called after him. 'Thank you, Lochty.'

Lochty acknowledged this with a wave, and then got into his car and drove off to have dinner with Jinette.

It took another fortnight for Kier to put his plan into action.

Finally, he was ready. He'd asked Iona to have dinner with him at his house, giving no hint of his plan. He knew she'd tell him she'd cycle there to save him from coming to pick her up in his car. She'd taken to using Jinette's bicycle, enjoying the summery weather, fresh air and sunshine. So he knew this is what she'd say. He accepted her offer to do this, for he wanted to set things up at the house. Something special. A surprise when she arrived.

He fussed with the dinner he had cooking in the oven. The wrong choice for a hot summer night, but the casserole was baking nicely and it smelled delicious. Cake and chocolates, courtesy of Gairn, were on a cake stand, and the tea and champagne were set on the kitchen table.

Kier went through to the living room to see if Lochty had finished stringing up the twinkle lights. The living room walls were painted pale grey and soft white, and watercolour paintings of his fields set in the winter matched the colour scheme.

'Thanks for helping me, Lochty. I hoped you still had the lights.'

'Happy to help you, Kier.'

Lochty finished pinning the lights up and flicked them on. 'There you go, all twinkly. Have you got the rose petals for scattering?'

Kier didn't reply. He just stood there thinking, his heart pounding.

'Are you okay?' Lochty asked him.

Kier shook his head. 'I'm nervous. I never feel like this.'

'Take three deep breaths...in and out,' Lochty advised.

Kier breathed in and out as instructed.

'Feel a bit better?'

'Yes, I do,' said Kier.

Lochty then looked at him. 'You're not wearing that casual blue shirt and jeans are you?'

Kier blinked. 'Yes, why?'

'No, no, that won't do. Away and change into one of your posh business outfits. Trousers, white shirt and silk tie. This is a special occasion. Make it look like you've made an effort.'

With a look of panic, realising he wasn't dressed well, Kier dashed off to his bedroom to get changed.

Lochty called through to him. 'Put a spurt on. Iona will be here soon.'

A couple of minutes later Kier emerged well–dressed. He stood in front of Lochty, as if for inspection, arms outstretched. 'How do I look?'

'That's better, but straighten your tie. It's squiffy. And have you got the ring?'

Kier straightened his tie, and took the small velvet box from his trouser pocket. 'Got it.' He opened it to check and showed it to Lochty.

Lochty had seen it several times due to Kier's anxiousness that he'd bought the right ring. One Iona would love. Hopefully she would love him too, but he was going for the same successful method that had worked for Lochty when he'd asked Jinette to marry him.

'It's a dazzler,' said Lochty. 'Different from Jinette's ring, but I managed to find out what type of ring Iona would like. Jinette doesn't even know why I was so keen to talk about engagement rings, but Iona went on about how she loves diamond cluster rings. And that is one sparkler of a ring.'

'It's definitely a diamond cluster, isn't it?' Kier asked anxiously.

'Yes, when I was planning Jinette's ring, I became an amateur expert on ladies engagement rings. That's a diamond flower cluster to be precise, set in a band of white gold.'

'Right. And it'll fit her?'

'Yes, because Iona wore Jinette's ring to make a wish and it fitted well. She's tried Jinette's ring on a couple of times so that Jinette can admire it from someone else's perspective. She loves that ring. So, anyway, we know it will fit.'

'I can always get it resized,' Kier assured himself.

'Calm the beans,' Lochty said, seeing Kier's nerves get the better of him again.

Kier nodded and did the deep breathing again. 'I never ever feel like this.'

'Women do that to you, especially when you love them more than anything.'

'Do you think she'll say yes?' Kier sounded stressed.

'I do. It's not as if you're asking her to marry you. You're asking her if she'd like to get engaged. Just as I did with Jinette. It worked.'

'It did. She said she'd marry you.'

'Bonus!' Lochty said, grinning.

Kier checked the time. 'She should be here soon.'

The doorbell rang. Kier and Lochty both jumped.

'She's early!' Kier hissed.

Lochty grabbed one of the boxes of rose petals and started to throw them around the living room floor. 'Quick, grab the other box and starting scattering.'

Kier threw the petals around like a man possessed while Lochty ran away.

'Good luck, Kier,' he shouted and scarpered out the kitchen door into the back garden and drove away.

Kier took a deep steadying breath and opened the front door to welcome Iona.

She wore a pretty blouse and skirt, and had brushed her hair silky smooth, and freshened her makeup after working at the shop all day.

'You look beautiful,' he said, stepping aside so she could come in.

'You look very smart.' She followed him as he led her through to the living room.

'Dinner smells tasty,' she remarked, and then she saw the twinkle lights...and the rose petals scattered over the floor...

She gazed at Kier.

'I wanted to ask you something,' he began.

She held her breath and gazed up at him, hardly daring to believe this was real.

'I know we've not actually dated, but, I think you must know how I feel about you, Iona.'

She stood there, blinking, overwhelmed. She really hadn't expected this. She'd thought they'd have dinner and he'd show her the autumnhouse he'd been building. And maybe they'd take things to another level. Maybe. Hopefully.

He took the ring box from his pocket and opened it.

Her eyes widened when she saw the most beautiful diamond cluster ring she'd ever seen.

He took a deep breath. 'I wondered if you'd like to get engaged?'

He stood there presenting the ring to her, hoping she'd accept.

She smiled, overwhelmed with a rush of emotions. And then she said, 'Yes. I'd love to marry you.'

Now he understood why Lochty had run out of Jinette's cottage cheering and punching the air with glee. Kier didn't run out of the house, but he did sweep Iona off her feet, lifting her up, cheering, smiling.

Then he put her down and slipped the ring on her finger, and kissed her, longingly, lovingly.

'I love you more than anyone, or anything. I've loved you since I first saw you.'

She gazed up at him. 'I love you too, Kier.'

He opened a bottle of champagne and they drank a toast to their engagement, their marriage, then he couldn't resist lifting her up again, sweeping her off her feet.

She laughed and kissed him, snuggling in, holding on tight as he carried her.

'I think we'll be happy together, Iona.'

She nodded and gazed at him lovingly. 'Yes, so do I.'

After dinner, he took her hand and led her out to the autumnhouse. 'What do you think? It's nearly finished.'

'I love it,' she said, stepping inside and gazing around. The scent of the garden mingled with the new chestnut wood, and there was a cosiness to it even though the windows were open.

'I'm going to add insulating blinds to the windows to keep it cosy for the winter months. But it'll look bright and fresh in the spring and summer mornings with the light shining in.' He indicated towards the roof. 'I'll add adequate lighting. You can advise what you want.'

'Me?'

'Yes, this is for you. Your autumnhouse where you can sit and sew your quilts during long autumn evenings, and decorate it with twinkle lights in the heart of the winter.' He looked around and nodded. 'It'll look great with the winter light pouring in during the day and the glow from the fields covered in snow.' He gazed at her and took her hands in his. Her ring sparkled in the evening light. 'I want you to have the autumnhouse, and add any furnishings, vintage, hand made, whatever you want.'

'I love it. I really think it's perfect.'

'I only hope that I'll be welcome to join you when you're not too busy sewing.'

'You'll always be welcome.' She hesitated. 'What about the sewing shop? What will happen to it?'

'I assumed you'd still want to keep the shop.'

'I do.'

'That's settled then.'

But not everything was settled. 'I still have my flat to deal with.'

'I'll take care of that. You won't need to go back. I'll have anything you want brought here.'

'There's nothing from my past that I left behind that I want.'

He gazed at her, his heart full of love and admiration for her.

She smiled at him. 'You once asked me if I could find a way to stay where I wanted to be, and not go back to whatever I wanted to leave behind. Now here I am with you.'

Kier smiled and pulled her close.

Iona noticed how sexy he looked. She was tempted to kiss him, and this time she did, leaning up and kissing the man she was going to marry.

He wrapped his arms around her and then indicated out one of the windows, at the fields of flowers, glowing in the burnished evening light. 'I saw a film once, and the couple got married in a field blooming with flowers. It looked so romantic, and I wondered...'

Iona gazed out at the fields, picturing taking her wedding vows amid all those beautiful flowers — and nodded. 'Yes, that would be perfect for us.'

Kier kissed her again and again, and then led her outside into the fields of flowers, lifting her up when she was almost waist–deep in the colouring blooms and greenery.

Then Kier's phone rang.

Iona nodded for him to take the call.

Kier smiled when he saw the caller ID. 'Hello, Lochty.'

'Well, what did Iona say? Did she say yes?' Lochty asked excitedly.

'She did. Iona says she'll marry me.'

The loud cheer from Lochty resounded in the warm night air. 'I can't wait to tell Jinette.'

Kier finished the call, clicked the phone off permanently for the remainder of the night, and swept Iona up into his arms.

She wrapped her arms around his shoulders and matched the passion of his kisses as the scent of the flowers all around them filled the warm summer night.

End

Embroidery Pattern

An embroidery pattern of The Sewing Shop, based on the book cover, is included here. It was designed by the author, De-ann Black.

You can download a printable version of the pattern from:
De-annBlack.com/ShopPattern

The pattern is also printed to scale on page 137 with instructions on pages 140 and 141.

The Sewing Shop Embroidery Pattern Instructions

Thread: use one or two strands of embroidery floss.

This design was sewn on white cotton fabric.

Hoop size: six inches.

Trace the pattern on to the fabric.

Stitch the shop's main outline, window and door.
Stitch the canopy and the shop's name.
Then finish by stitching the items in the window.

Canopy
Pink & white - satin stitch.

Shop
Pink outline - back stitch.

Shop Name
Black - back stitch.

Window frame
Pink - back stitch.
Pale grey shelf - back stitch.

Door
Pink outlines - back stitch.
Pink letterbox & door handle - satin stitch.
Grey doorsign - straight stitch.

Cake stand
Pale grey - back stitch.

Cupcakes
Pink & blue bases - satin stitch.
White topping - satin stitch.
Red cherries - single stitch.

Cakes
Pink, white & pale vanilla - satin stitch.
White, pink & pale chocolate - satin stitch.

Bunting
Pink & White - back stitch & satin stitch.

Large rolls of fabric
Pink & lilac - satin stitch.

Small rolls of fabric
Blue, pale yellow & pink - satin stitch.

Button jar
Jar outline pale grey - back stitch.
Pink top - satin stitch.
Pink, blue & yellow buttons - French knots.

Quilt
Pink binding/outline - back stitch.
Pink, blue & lilac patchwork squares - satin stitch.
Pale grey ties - single stitch.

Dress & stand
Pink dress - satin stitch.
Black stand - single stitch.

Sewing machine
Pink - back stitch & satin stitch.
Grey needle - single stitch.

About the Author:

Follow De-ann on Instagram @deann.black

De-ann Black is a bestselling author, scriptwriter and former newspaper journalist. She has over 80 books published. Romance, crime thrillers, espionage novels, action adventure. And children's books (non-fiction rocket science books and children's fiction). She became an Amazon All-Star author in 2014 and 2015.

She previously worked as a full-time newspaper journalist for several years. She had her own weekly columns in the press. This included being a motoring correspondent where she got to test drive cars every week for the press for three years.

Before being asked to work for the press, De-ann worked in magazine editorial writing everything from fashion features to social news. She was the marketing editor of a glossy magazine. She is also a professional artist and illustrator. Fabric design, dressmaking, sewing, knitting and fashion are part of her work.

Additionally, De-ann has always been interested in fitness, and was a fitness and bodybuilding champion, 100 metre runner and mountaineer. As a former N.A.B.B.A. Miss Scotland, she had a weekly fitness show on the radio that ran for over three years.

De-ann trained in Shukokai karate, boxing, kickboxing, Dayan Qigong and Jiu Jitsu. She is currently based in Scotland.
Her colouring books and embroidery design books are available in paperback. These include Floral Nature Embroidery Designs and Scottish Garden Embroidery Designs.

Also by De-ann Black (Romance, Action/Thrillers & Children's books). See her Amazon Author page or website for further details about her books, screenplays, illustrations, art and fabric designs.
www.De-annBlack.com

Romance books:

Sewing, Crafts & Quilting series:
1. The Sewing Bee
2. The Sewing Shop

Quilting Bee & Tea Shop series:
1. The Quilting Bee
2. The Tea Shop by the Sea

Heather Park: Regency Romance

Snow Bells Haven series:
1. Snow Bells Christmas
2. Snow Bells Wedding

Summer Sewing Bee
Christmas Cake Chateau

Cottages, Cakes & Crafts series:
1. The Flower Hunter's Cottage
2. The Sewing Bee by the Sea
3. The Beemaster's Cottage
4. The Chocolatier's Cottage
5. The Bookshop by the Seaside
6. The Dressmaker's Cottage

Sewing, Knitting & Baking series:
1. The Tea Shop
2. The Sewing Bee & Afternoon Tea
3. The Christmas Knitting Bee
4. Champagne Chic Lemonade Money
5. The Vintage Sewing & Knitting Bee

The Tea Shop & Tearoom series:
1. The Christmas Tea Shop & Bakery
2. The Christmas Chocolatier
3. The Chocolate Cake Shop in New York at Christmas
4. The Bakery by the Seaside
5. Shed in the City

Tea Dress Shop series:
1. The Tea Dress Shop At Christmas
2. The Fairytale Tea Dress Shop In Edinburgh
3. The Vintage Tea Dress Shop In Summer

Christmas Romance series:
1. Christmas Romance in Paris.
2. Christmas Romance in Scotland.

Romance, Humour, Mischief series:
1. Oops! I'm the Paparazzi
2. Oops! I'm A Hollywood Agent
3. Oops! I'm A Secret Agent
4. Oops! I'm Up To Mischief

The Bitch-Proof Suit series:
1. The Bitch-Proof Suit
2. The Bitch-Proof Romance
3. The Bitch-Proof Bride

The Cure For Love
Dublin Girl
Why Are All The Good Guys Total Monsters?
I'm Holding Out For A Vampire Boyfriend

Action/Thriller books:
Love Him Forever
Someone Worse
Electric Shadows
The Strife Of Riley
Shadows Of Murder
Cast a Dark Shadow

149

Children's books:
Faeriefied
Secondhand Spooks
Poison-Wynd
Wormhole Wynd
Science Fashion
School For Aliens

Colouring books:
Flower Nature
Summer Garden
Spring Garden
Autumn Garden
Sea Dream
Festive Christmas
Christmas Garden
Christmas Theme
Flower Bee
Wild Garden
Faerie Garden Spring
Flower Hunter
Stargazer Space
Bee Garden
Scottish Garden Seasons

Embroidery Design books:
Floral Nature Embroidery Designs
Scottish Garden Embroidery Designs

Printed in Great Britain
by Amazon